W9-CDT-138

The Fabulous Sinkhole and Other Stories

Jesús Salvador Treviño

Arte Público Press
Houston, Texas
1995

This volume is made possible through grants from the National Endowment for the Arts (a federal agency), the Lila Wallace-Reader's Digest Fund, and the Andrew W. Mellon Foundation.

Recovering the past, creating the future

Arte Público Press
University of Houston
Houston, Texas 77204-2090

Cover design by Mark Piñón

Original art "The Fabulous Sinkhole"
by Wayne Alaniz Healy

About the Artist

Wayne Alaniz Healy is a muralist and director of East Los Streetscapers, the public art team. Mr. Healy's imagery celebrates Chicano culture and has been exhibited internationally. The monoprint used for this cover design was created at Self Help Graphics Print Studio in East Los Angeles.

Treviño, Jesús Salvador,
      The fabulous sinkhole and other stories / by Jesús Treviño.
            p.   cm.
      ISBN 1-55885-129-1
      1. Mexican Americans—California—Los Angeles—Social life and customs—Fiction. 2. Los Angeles (Calif.)—Social life and customs—Fiction. I. Title.
PS3570.R445F33   1995
813'.54—dc20   94-39234
                                                      CIP

For Bobbi

Contents

The Fabulous Sinkhole
and Other Stories

The Fabulous Sinkhole

The Fabulous Sinkhole

The hole in Mrs. Romero's front yard erupted with the thunderous whoosh of a pent-up volcano, sending a jet of water dancing eight feet into the air. It stood there for a moment, shimmering in the sun like a crystal skyscraper, before it fell back on itself and settled into a steady trickle of water emanating from the earth.

The gurgling water made a soft, sonorous sound, not unlike music, as it quickly spread, inundating the low lawn surrounding the sculpted hole, painting a swirling mosaic of leaves, twigs, and dandelion puffs.

Pages of the weekly *Arroyo Bulletin News* were swept up by the fast moving water, creating a film of literary discourse that floated on the surface of the water before becoming soaked and eventually sinking into the whirlpool created by the unusual hole.

Within moments of the unexpected appearance of the geyser, the serenity of Mrs. Romero's ordinary, predictable world was disrupted. On that Saturday morning Mrs. Romero's life, and that of the other residents of Arroyo Grande, a border town along the Rio Grande river, was forever transformed by an event as mysterious as the immaculate conception and as unexpected as summer snow.

The routine of Mrs. Romero's Saturday mornings—the leisurely watering of her philodendrons, Creeping Charlies and spider plants, the radio recipe hour, and the morning *telenovelas*—evaporated the moment that she stepped out the back door to feed Junior, her three-year old poodle-Afghan mix.

No sooner had she opened the door to the back yard, than the dog, whom she let sleep in the house with her, caught whiff of something and ran around to the front of the house. He bounded back in a moment and began to jump, yelp, whine, bark and engage in other canine theatrics to draw Mrs. Romero's attention to something unusual that was happening in her front yard.

"*¿Qué trae ese perro?*" Mrs. Romero asked herself as she circled her house and walked out to the front of her modest stucco home. She then saw that Junior was barking at a hole in her front yard.

The hole was about three feet in diameter. It was located ten feet from the white picket fence that framed her front yard and a few yards from the cement walkway leading from her porch to the sidewalk.

As she walked down the porch steps, she noticed the most pleasant vanilla odor in the air. "*Qué bonito huele,*" she thought to herself.

She started to waddle across the lawn, but saw that it was flooded and opted to use the cement walkway instead. When she got to the point on the walkway that was closest to the hole, she stooped over to examine the depression and noticed that there was water bubbling up from the earth.

Mrs. Romero's first thought was that some of the neighborhood kids had dug the hole during the night. "*Chavalos traviesos,*" she surmised. But when she saw that there was water coming up from the ground, she had second thoughts about this being the mischievous work of local juveniles.

Where was the water coming from? Perhaps it was a broken water main. Just then, a clump of grass fell into the hole as it expanded further. The hole seemed to be growing.

"*Qué raro,*" she said as she stood up.

Mrs. Romero was not someone easily buffaloed by much of anything in her long and eventful life. She had weathered the deportations of the Thirties (eventually returning to Arroyo Grande by foot, thank you), the Second World War, six children (all living), sixteen grandchildren, three husbands (deceased), four wisdom-tooth extractions, an appendectomy, the Blizzard of '52, an Internal Revenue audit, and weekly assaults on her privacy by Jehovah's Witnesses.

She was not about to be bamboozled by a mere hole in the ground.

She walked into her house and returned with a broom, which she proceeded to stick into the hole, handle first, to see if she could determine how far down the hole went.

When the broom handle had gone in to the point where she was holding the broom by the straw whiskers, she gave up and pulled the broom out. "What a big hole," she said out loud.

About this time, thirteen-year-old Reymundo Salazar, who lived in the adjacent block and was well known for the notorious spitball he pitched for the Arroyo Grande Sluggers, happened to be walking by Mrs. Romero's house on his way to Saturday morning baseball practice. Seeing Mrs. Romero taking the stick out of the hole in the lawn, he stopped and asked what was up.

"*Mira, m'ijo*," she said. "Come look at this hole that just now appeared *aquí en mi patio.*"

Reymundo opened the gate and entered the yard, scratching Junior under his left ear. The dog by now had forgotten the mystery of the hole and was trying to get up a game of ball with the boy.

"Did you dig this hole, Señora?" Reymundo asked.

"No, *m'ijo*, that's the way I found it," Mrs. Romero said, somewhat defensively. She wiped her wet hands on the apron that circled her ample midriff and shook her head in wonder. "Look, it's getting bigger."

Sure enough, as Reymundo and Mrs. Romero watched, another large clump of earth fell into the hole as more and more water bubbled up from the earth below.

"You'd better get a plumber, Señora," advised Reymundo as he started back to the sidewalk, "It's probably a broken water pipe."

"*Ay Dios mío*," said Mrs. Romero, shaking her head once again. "If it's not one thing it's another."

As he walked away, Reymundo, who had been raised by his mother to be polite to older people, thought he'd compliment Mrs. Romero for the wonderful smell which permeated the air. He assumed it came from something she had dowsed herself with. "Nice perfume you're wearing, Mrs. Romero," he called out to her. "Smells real nice!"

O O O

Within an hour, news of the hole in Mrs. Romero's front yard had spread throughout Arroyo Grande as neighbors from as far away as Mercado and Seventh Street came to see the sight. Mrs. Romero's next-door neighbors, Juan and Eugenia Alaniz, were the first over.

Mrs. Romero explained the appearance of the strange hole to the couple, and Juan said he'd see what he could find out. He went back to his garage and returned with a long metallic pole with which he began to plumb the depths of the sinkhole. Like young Reymundo, he was certain it was a broken water pipe and thought he might locate it with the metal pole.

But after much probing, and getting his worn Kinney casuals soaked, Juan reported back to Mrs. Romero that he could find no pipes under her yard. "Beats me," he said.

By now the hole had enlarged to about six feet across. More and more water kept bubbling up, undermining the earth around the edges of the hole until eventually another bit of the lawn went into the hole. It appeared to sink to a bottom. Juan Alaniz extended his twenty-foot measuring tape to its full length and stuck it into the hole and still it did not hit bottom.

"It's deep," he said authoritatively to Mrs. Romero and his wife Eugenia, showing them the twenty-foot mark on the measuring tape. "Real deep."

"*Qué bonito huele*," said Eugenia. "Smells like orange blossoms."

"No," said Juan, "smells like bread pudding. You know, *capirotada*."

"Yes," said Mrs. Romero. "I noticed the smell, too. But it smells like vanilla to me. No?"

"Cherry-flavored tobacco," said grumpy, Old Man Baldemar, who had crossed the street to see what the commotion was about. "It definitely smells of cherry-flavored tobacco."

Old Man Baldemar was known on the block for his foul mouth and his dislike of the neighborhood kids. He seldom spoke to anyone, kept to himself, and most people just stayed clear of him. That he would go out of his way to be social was just another indication of the deep feelings the hole stirred in those who saw it.

While Mrs. Romero and her neighbors discussed the powerful aroma that came from the hole, Reymundo Salazar returned from the baseball field along with the members of the Arroyo Grande Sluggers. They descended on Mrs. Romero's on their skateboards, looking like a swarm of fighter planes coming down *Calle Cuatro*. Reymundo had told his friends about the doings at Mrs. Romero's, and all were eager to see the mysterious water hole.

"Maybe it goes all the way to China!" Reymundo joked as he came to a stop in front of the white picket fence that surrounded Mrs. Romero's yard.

"Nah, a hole can't go all the way through the earth," said twelve-year old Yoli Mendoza, taking it all very seriously as she finished off a perfect street-to-sidewalk ollie and came to a stop next to him. Yoli was advanced for her age, a real brain at school, and the tomboy of the group. She never missed a chance to show the boys in the neighborhood that she knew more about most things than they did, or that she could outskate them.

"In the center of the earth there's thick molten rock," she said professorially. "The *magma* and nothing can get through it—not even this hole."

At this point, chubby Bobby Hernández, also twelve years old but nowhere near Yoli's intellect, started arguing with Yoli, hoping to browbeat her into admitting that it *was* possible for a hole to extend from Mrs. Romero's yard all the way to China.

"Itcanitcanitcanitcanitcan," he said, as if repeating it enough times would make it so.

"You are an ignoramus and a lout," Yoli said emphatically, adjusting the ribbon at the end of her ponytail, "and not worth the time it takes to argue with you."

"Maybe we'd better call the Department of Water and Power," said Juan Alaniz as he examined the hole. "I'll do that and see if they can't get somebody out here. After all, it's water—they should know what to do."

While Juan went off to his house to place the call, Eugenia and Old Man Baldemar stayed to talk to Mrs. Romero. Meanwhile, other neighbors on *Calle Cuatro* were beginning to gather to see what all the commotion was about.

Mrs. Domínguez, the neighborhood gossip, who had spied the crowd forming down the street and presumed there had been a car accident, immediately called Sally Mendez and Doña Cuca Tanguma and told them to meet her at Mrs. Romero's. When the three arrived and found there was no accident but only an ever-widening water hole, Mrs. González was only momentarily embarrassed.

"Why, this is much better than an accident," she said to her friends as she regained her composure, "because no one's been hurt."

Miguelito Pérez, driving to work at the Copa de Oro restaurant bar, pulled his '73 Chevy over when he saw the crowd on *Calle Cuatro*, and got out to investigate. Within moments he, too, was integrated into the crowd.

"Hey, Señora Romero," he said, pointing to the picket fence that separated the expanding hole from the cement sidewalk. "If this hole continues to grow, it's going to wreck your fence."

Don Sabastiano Diamante, an expatriate Spaniard who laced his conversation with Biblical quotations and aphorisms, heard the commotion as far away as *Calle Diez*. He found the long walk to Mrs. Romero's rewarded by an ideal opportunity to dazzle a few more souls with his knowledge of the Good Book. He was always quick to point out how the scriptures neatly underscored the socialist ideals that had led him in and out of the Spanish Civil War and eventually brought him to Arroyo Grande.

"*And God said, Let the waters under the heaven be gathered together unto one place,*" Don Sabastiano quoted as he walked his Dachshund Peanuts slowly around the body of water, "*and the gathering together of waters he called the Seas.* Genesis One, Ten"

Choo Choo Torres, who would later give an account of the day's events to his sixth-grade class during the afternoon "Tell-a-Story" hour, arrived early on with the other Sluggers and made a list of the people who visited Mrs. Romero's front yard on that day.

Among the five pages of names that Choo-Choo Torres painstakingly compiled were: Old Man Baldemar, Don Carlos Valdez, Ed Carillo, Eddie Martinez, Cha Cha Mendiola, Juan and Eugenia Alaniz, Raúl and Simón Maldonado, Braulio Armendáriz, Pablo Figueroa, Raoul Cervantes, Sam Bedford (from the City Bureau of Public Works), the Méndez family (six in all), the Márquez Family (father and three kids), the Baca family (four in all), the Armenta family (eight in all), the Arroyo Grande Sluggers (eleven kids in all, including Reymundo Salazar, Bobby Hernández, Tudí Domínguez, Choo-Choo Torres, Beto Méndez, Robert and Johnnie

Rodríguez, Junior Valdez, Smiley Rojas, Jeannie De La Cruz, and, of course, Yoli Mendoza), Howard Meltzer (the milkman), Chato Pastoral, Kiki Sánchez, Richard and Diane Mumm (visiting from Iowa), Mrs. Ybarra, Mrs. Domínguez, Sally Méndez, Doña Cuca Tanguma, Dr. Claude S. Fischer (who was conducting a sociological survey of barrio residents), Rolando Hinojosa, Miguelito Pérez, Rosalinda Rodríguez, Mr. and Mrs. Alejandro Morales, Charles Allen (who connected Arroyo Grande homes with cable TV), Lefty Ramírez, the Cisneros family (nine in all), Don Sabastiano Diamante and his dog Peanuts, Julia Miranda, One-eyed Juan Lara, Sylvia Morales, Rusty Gómez (from the Department of Water and Power), David Sandoval, Max Martínez, 'Lil Louie Ruiz, Rudy 'Bugs' Vargas, Pete Navarro, Bobby Lee and Yolanda Verdugo, The Torres family (four not counting Choo-Choo), Elvis Presley, Ritchie Valens, César Chávez, Frida Kahlo, John F. Kennedy, Che Guevara, Michael Jackson, and Pee Wee Herman.

The last several names, of course, were scoffed at by Choo Choo's classmates. Yoli Mendoza, who sat two seats behind Choo Choo, lost no time in openly accusing him of being a big fat liar, to which the other classmates joined in with a chorus of "yeahs" and "orales."

Truth to tell, Choo Choo had gotten a bit carried away with his list-making, but didn't see any need to admit his minor human idiosyncrasies to riff-raff the likes of his classmates.

With brazen, dead-pan bravado that—years later—would serve him in good stead at the poker table, Choo Choo insisted that each and every one of the people on his list had been at Mrs. Romero's house that day, and that he had personally seen them with his own two eyes.

Had it been a weekday with everyone off to work, the crowd that gathered in front of Mrs. Romero's might not have been very big. But it was a Saturday morning, and quite a warm, sunny day at that. An ideal day for neighbors to come together and get caught up on each other's lives. And that they did.

By eleven o'clock that morning the crowd in front of Mrs. Romero's yard was easily over fifty people and growing bigger and bigger by the hour.

For Mrs. Romero it was quite a delight. She had not had so many visitors in years, not since her husband Maclovio had passed away. Her husband's death had taken the spark out of Mrs. Romero's life—they had been married for thirty-six years—and no matter what her daughters, son, and grandchildren tried to do to cheer her up, her laughter always seemed forced and her smile polite. There were some who said she was merely biding time waiting to join her husband. Her children, caught up in their own lives, came to visit less and less frequently. On the day of the sinkhole, it had been a long month since she had been visited by anyone.

But now, hearing the lively chatter from her neighbors, she wondered why she hadn't made more of an effort to get out and meet people *herself*.

She felt warmed by the company of her neighbors and the cheerful sound of their laughter. Then and there she resolved that from now on she'd make it a point to visit her neighbors on a regular basis and would demand that her children and grandchildren visit more often. "*Va!*" she thought to herself, "I'm not in the grave yet."

Tony Valdez, who ran the corner store, heard about the crowd gathering at Mrs. Romero's, and his money-making mind immediately sprang into action. He sent his son Junior, who made the mistake of returning from baseball practice to tell his dad about the doings at Mrs. Romero's, to the location with a grocery cart full of cold Cokes.

Before long a *tamalero*, a *paletero*, and a fruit vendor had joined the boy, and all were doing brisk business in front of Mrs. Romero's house.

By noon there was quite a festive air to the day as neighbors sipped Cokes, munched *tamales*, chomped on popsicles, and carried on the kind of conversation they normally reserved for weddings and funerals. Old friendships were renewed, new friends made, and, in general, more gossip and telephone numbers exchanged that day than had been exchanged in months.

One-Eyed Juan Lara stopped to examine the crowd at the ever-widening hole and speculated that if the hole got any bigger, Mrs. Romero could charge admission for the neighborhood kids to swim in it.

"You'll have your own swimming pool, *señora*," he said, "just like the *ricos*."

Frank Del Roble, who had grown up on *Calle Cuatro* and now worked as a reporter for the *real* town newspaper, the *Arroyo Daily Times*, overheard Don Luis and countered that this probably wasn't such a good idea. "If this water is coming from a broken sewer line," he said, "the water might be contaminated, might get people sick."

"But look how clear it is," Juan Lara replied, pointing to the bubbling aperture.

Frank had to admit that the water flooding Mrs. Romero's front lawn was quite clear and not at all looking like a sewage spill.

Frank had been driving to the office when he had seen the crowd gathered outside Mrs. Romero's and had gotten out to investigate. Now, he pulled out his trusty spiral notepad and began taking notes.

Bobby Hernández, meanwhile, was still contending that the hole went all the way to China, and Yoli was still arguing back that he was crazy, an ignoramus, and going against accepted scientific fact.

Bobby wasn't sure what an ignoramus was, but was damned if he was going to ask Yoli about it.

About this time a large "plop" sound announced the arrival of the first of many items that would bubble up in Mrs. Romero's front yard that day.

"Look!" Bobby said smugly, pointing to the hole. "I told you so!"

All heads turned to the hole and a hush fell over the group of spectators as they stared in wonder at the item floating on top of the water.

To Yoli's astonishment and Bobby's delight it was a large, straw hat, pointed in the center, not unlike those worn by millions of Chinese people halfway around the world.

○ ○ ○

"No, it's not a broken pipe," said Rusty Gómez, who worked for the Department of Water and Power and had been sent over to investigate the commotion on *Calle Cuatro*. He had measured and prodded the watery hole for half an hour before announcing to the sizeable group gathered at Mrs. Romero's his conclusion.

"What you have here," he said, "is a sinkhole!"

A murmur coursed through the crowd as they played the new word on their lips.

"What's a sinkhole?" Mrs. Romero asked. She was determined to know all about this thing that had disrupted her day and was creating such ever-widening chaos in her yard.

"It's a kind of depression in the ground; it caves in when undermined by water from an underground river or stream. You don't know its there until the ground gives way and the water surfaces."

"Yeah?" said Juan Alaniz cautiously. "So where's the river?"

"Years ago," continued Rusty, "there used to be an *arroyo* going through this neighborhood, right along *Calle Cuatro*. When it rained, a good-sized stream used to run through here, right down to the Rio Grande. There's probably an underground stream someplace and that's where this water is coming from."

"That," Rusty mused, "or an underground cavern connecting to the Rio Grande itself. Hell, it's only a half mile away. Yeah, I'd say this water's coming from the Rio Grande."

"Well what can I do about it?" Mrs. Romero asked.

"Don't know, *señora*. If I were you, I'd call the City Bureau of Public Works. They've got an engineering department. This is more their field of work. Say what is that, a bird cage?" Rusty Gómez pointed to the sinkhole where a shiny aluminum bird cage had suddenly popped up from the ground.

Old Man Baldemar, who lived alone in a single-room converted garage, and whose only companions were two parakeets which he had named *el gordo y el flaco*, fished the bird cage out of the water.

"*Señora* Romero," he said. "If you don't mind, I'd like to keep this here bird cage. The one I have for my *pajaritos* just this morning rusted through in the bottom. Those birds will get a real kick out of this."

"*Cómo no, Señor Baldemar*," Mrs. Romero replied. "If you can use it, *pos* take it!" And that is how the first of the articles that popped into Mrs. Romero's front yard was taken away by one of the residents of Arroyo Grande.

Within an hour, more and more items began to float to the surface of the sinkhole, now about fifteen feet across. Choo Choo, Reymundo, Yoli, Bobby, and the rest of the neighborhood kids kept themselves busy by pulling objects out of the sinkhole and laying them on the sidewalk to dry.

Frank del Roble, who had already gotten a couple of quotes from Mrs. Romero for the piece he was now sure he'd write on the event at *Calle Cuatro*, stooped over the sidewalk and started making a list of the artifacts.

Throughout the day, Frank kept a careful record of the items that came bubbling up through Mrs. Romero's sinkhole, and this is what the list looked like:

* a brown fedora, size 7½,
fourteen football player cards, three of Joe Montana,
one baseball player card of Babe Ruth,
a Gideon bible,
a pair of plastic 3-D glasses,
a paperback edition of Webster's dictionary,
three paperback science-fiction novels,
four Teenage Mutant Turtle comic books,
a baseball bat,
three baseball gloves, one of them for a left-hander,
one basketball,
fourteen golf balls,
four unopened cans of semi-gloss paint primer,
an aluminum bird cage,
a 1975 world globe,
a tuba,
a yellow plastic flyswatter,
one yard of blue ribbon,
a toy magnifying glass,
a 1965 Smith Corona typewriter,
an April, 1994 issue of *Art News* magazine,
a July 16, 1965 issue of *Life* magazine,
an August, 1988 issue of *Life* magazine,
a July 4, 1969 issue of *Time* magazine,
the *Los Angeles Times* for October 9, 1932,
an issue of *TV Guide* magazine for the week of April
     18-23, 1988
an unused package of condoms,
a blank certificate of merit,
fourteen Mexican coins of various denominations,
a three peso Cuban note,
$3.17 in U.S. currency including a silver dollar,
a 500 Yen note,
a size 14.5 steel-belted Goodyear radial tire,
the frame of a black, 1949 Chevy Fleetline,
a New York Mets baseball cap,
a deck of Hoyle playing cards with the ten of clubs
     and the three of diamonds missing,
a finely crafted silver pin,
a brochure for travel to *Macchu Picchu*,
a claw-toothed hammer,
three screwdrivers,

a pair of compasses,
a ruler,
a leatherbound copy of *David Copperfield*,
three pairs of jeans,
sixteen shirts of different kinds, sizes and colors,
a white terry-cloth robe with the initials RR on it,
eight sets of men and women's shoes,
a broken Mickey Mouse watch,
a 14K gold wedding band,
a bronze belt buckle,
a fake pearl broach,
a tambourine,
three empty wine bottles made of green glass,
an orange pet food dish,
a wooden walking cane with a dragon carved on the
     handle,
two umbrellas, one bright red and one yellow with
     brown stripes,
a 20-foot extension cord,
32 empty soft-drink bottles of assorted brands,
a pair of Zeitz binoculars,
a mint set of U.S. postage stamps commemorating
     rock and roll/rhythm and blues,
a Max Factor makeup kit,
five brand new #2 pencils,
a Parker fountain pen,
four ball-point pens,
a set of ceramic wind chimes,
six pairs of sunglasses, one with a lens missing,
the figures of Mary, the baby Jesus, Joseph and a
     camel from a porcelain nativity scene,
a framed autographed photo of Carmen Miranda,
a bag of clothespins,
a three-speed Schwinn bicycle with one wheel miss-
     ing,
six size C Duracell batteries,
six record albums: *La Jaula de Oro* by Los Tigres del
     Norte, a collection of "Top Hits from 1957," a
     Sesame Street Singalong album, an album by
     The Jackson Five, "Learn to Mambo with Pérez
     Prado," and The Beatles' white album,

A black and red Inter-Galactic lasergun with accompanying black plastic communicator and extraterrestrial voice-decoder,
a sturdy, wooden push broom with a large bristle head,
an 8 x 10 wooden frame,
a red brick,
a map of Belkin County, Texas,
a book of Mexican proverbs,
a desk stapler,
two large black and white fuzzy dice,
a plastic swizzle stick with a conga dancer at one end, a rounded ball at the other end, and "Havana Club" printed along its side,
a subway token,
a red and white packet of love potion labeled "*Medicina de Amor*,"
a 5 x 7 artist sketch pad,
five auto hubcaps, four of them matching,
a St. Christopher's medal,
a 4-inch metal replica of the Eiffel Tower,
a New York auto license,
a large ring of assorted keys,
a plastic hoola-hoop, and lastly,
a Chinese sun hat.

As curious as Frank's exhaustive list was, the fact is that by the end of the day every single article had found a home in the hands of one or another of the people who stopped by Mrs. Romero's.

In quite a number of cases, the article seemed ideally suited for the person who picked it up. Like Old Man Baldemar walking away with a new bird cage for the one that had broken that morning, or Miguelito Pérez finding a hub cap to replace the one he had lost the week previous. Alejandro Morales found a red brick with the company name "Simons" embossed on it, and was inspired to use it as the centerpiece for the new brick front porch he was adding to his house.

In other cases, the link between what a person took away from the sinkhole and a particular need in their life was not apparent at all.

Tudí Domínguez, for example, walked away from Mrs. Romero's having collected all 32 soft drink bottles and intending to return them to a recycling center for the rebate.

But on the way home he ran into Marcy Stone, a blond-haired, blue-eyed *gringita* on whom he had a devastating crush, and, rather than be seen carrying the bag of empty bottles, dumped them in a nearby trash can. The bottles never surfaced again.

Marcy continued to ignore Tudi throughout 6th and 7th grade until her family moved out of town, and Tudi grew up to be a used-car salesman. Never once did he ever think of the coke bottles he abandoned that day, nor were any of the four wives he married in the course of his otherwise uneventful life either blond or blue-eyed.

For most people at Mrs. Romero's, it wouldn't be until weeks, months, or even years later that they would associate an item they had carried off from the sinkhole on that peculiar Saturday with a specific influence in their lives.

By one o'clock, the sinkhole had undermined the earth on which Mrs. Romero's white picket fence was built and, just as Miguelito Pérez has predicted, the fence, pickets and all, plopped into the water.

Juan Alaniz helped Miguelito pull the picket fence out as a favor to *la señora*, and they neatly stacked the broken sections of the fence on her front porch.

Sam Bedford, from the City Bureau of Public Works, finally showed up at two o'clock that afternoon.

The balding, city employee was grumpy because his afternoon game of golf had been disrupted by an emergency call to see about potholes on Fourth Street.

"Well that's definitely more than a pothole," Sam said, whistling in astonishment at the sinkhole which now measured twenty feet across.

By now the neighborhood kids had collected several dozen items and had them neatly drying on the sidewalk in front of Mrs. Romero's house.

The crowd now numbered about a hundred people as neighbors continued to call friends and relatives to see the unusual event.

Sam strutted about the hole for about an hour, comparing the yard and the street with several city maps and sewage charts he carried under his arm. Now and then he'd say "uh-huh" or "yeah," as if carrying on a deep conversation with himself.

Finally he returned to Mrs. Romero's porch where the elderly woman sat sipping lemonade with Mrs. Domínguez, Sally Méndez, and Doña Cuca Tanguma.

"Don't know what to tell you, lady," Sam said, putting his maps away. "It sure looks like a sinkhole, though I've never seen one so large. We won't be able to do anything about it till Monday. I'll put in a request for a maintenance crew to come out here first thing."

"But what about in the meantime?" Mrs. Romero asked.

Sam just shook his head. "Sorry, I can't help you. Just keep people away so no one falls in." As he walked away he noticed something amid the pile of junk that was accumulating on the sidewalk. "Oh, by the way," he continued, "Do you mind if I take some of those golf balls laying over there?"

○ ○ ○

If there were two incidents that would be remembered by everyone on the day of Mrs. Romero's sinkhole, it was the argument between Father Ronquillo and his parishioner, Señora Florencia Ybarra, and the appearance of the largest item to pop out of the sinkhole, something that occupied the concentrated energy of five well-built young men and a tow truck for over an hour.

The Father Ronquillo incident began innocently enough when Mrs. Ybarra, whose devotion to the Blessed Mother was renowned, saw a Gideon Bible pop out of the sinkhole. She fished it out of the water and found, to her amazement, that although the leatherette cover of the book was wet, when she opened it up, the inside pages were on the whole pretty dry.

She examined the Bible carefully and came to a conclusion she immediately shared with her assembled neighbors.

"It's a miracle!" she said, waving the Bible in the air. "Look, *la Santa Biblia* is dry! This water hole is a sign from the Lord and this Bible proves it!"

Mrs. Domínguez, and several other women gathered about Mrs. Ybarra to examine the Bible. They all agreed that the Bible, though damp, should have been soaked and that some divine intervention was not out of the question.

What capped the argument was the sudden appearance of a porcelain figure of Mary from a nativity scene, followed in swift succession by a porcelain baby Jesus and a porcelain Joseph.

"*Milagro!*" The mummur spread through the crowd.

Father Ronquillo, dressed in his work-out sweats and out on his morning jog, happened by Mrs. Romero's at precisely this moment. The crowd spent little time ushering him to the sinkhole to witness for himself the Holy Bible and figurines of the Blessed Mother, Joseph, and the baby Jesus that had miraculously appeared in the water.

"Oh, thank God you are here, Father." Mrs. Ybarra said. "Look, it's a miracle!"

The parish priest was silent for a moment as he examined the figures and the still widening sinkhole. He listened to Rusty Gómez's explanation of the sinkhole, then talked with Sam Bedford, then listened once again to Mrs. Ybarra, and then examined the figurines.

He hadn't counted on facing a theological debate on his morning jog, but was only too eager to responsibly shoulder his life work when the challenge presented itself.

"Well, there's certainly nothing miraculous about this," he said, pointing to the underside of the figures. "Look, it says J.C. Penney." He passed the figurines around for everyone to examine and, sure enough, the store name was printed on price labels stuck to the underside of each figurine.

"Of course it's no miracle," Frank Del Roble said emphatically as he compiled his list of the objects assembled on the sidewalk. Frank's university education had trained him to loathe superstitious people. "It's what keeps the *barrio* down," he was often heard to say. "Superstition and religion and no respect for science."

He surveyed the sizeable collection laid out on the sidewalk. "I think Rusty's right. This stuff's probably been dragged here by some underground current of the Rio Grande. There's a scientific explanation for everything."

"It's from South America, that's what!" said Bobby Hernández. "The Rio Grande is connected to the Amazon. I betcha all these things come from down South!"

"The Rio Grande definitely does *not* connect to the Amazon," Yoli countered, only too eager to show off her knowledge of geography. "The Rio Grande starts in Colorado and empties into the Atlantic Ocean in the Gulf of Mexico."

"It *is* connected to the Amazon," Bobby replied, secretly convinced that Yoli made up the facts that she announced with such authority. "Itisitisitisitisitis!"

"*Es un cuerno de abundancia*," said Don Sabastiano. "It's a cornucopia bringing something for everyone here."

"Definitely the Rio Grande," Juan Alaniz said, ignoring Don Sabastiano and nodding to Father Ronquillo. "That would explain where all this stuff is coming from."

He picked up a silver dollar from the collection of artifacts laid out on the sidewalk and flipped it in the air.
"All this stuff is probably from some junk yard up river."

Father Ronquillo, however, was not eager to allow
the faith of his parishioners to be dispelled so easily.
After all, if their faith was allowed to be undermined on
these little matters, where would it end?

"There is a scientific explanation for everything," he
agreed, examining a 20-foot extension cord that had
been drying on the sidewalk. He remembered that the
parish needed one.

"But remember that our Lord invented science." He
turned to the crowd around him and assumed his best
clerical demeanor, at least the best he could dressed in
jogging sweats.

"All of this may come from some junk yard," he said,
putting the extension cord under the elastic of his jogging pants, "but that doesn't mean that some higher
power did not arrange for all of this to happen."

"Then it *is* a miracle," said Mrs. Ybarra feeling vin-
dicated.

"For those who believe, there will always be mira-
cles," he said with reassuring eloquence. "And those
unfortunate souls so tainted by the cynicism of the
world that they cannot believe," he eyed Frank Del
Roble pointedly, "are only the lesser for it."

"I still think that all this stuff is coming from South
America," said Bobby, not giving up.

"I must prepare for the afternoon Mass," Father
Ronquillo said, moving through the crowd and back on
his running route. "Mrs. Romero," he said as he passed
her, "you should call the city to see about filling in this
hole before it does much more damage."

Indeed by now the hole had expanded to the edge of
the walkway and sidewalk. There, the cement had put a
halt to its growth. But on the far side of the yard, where
there was no cement, the hole had gone on a gluttonous
rampage, devouring so much of Mrs. Romero's front

yard that when Don Sabastiano paced off the hole it measured fully forty feet across. It was enormous by any standard. It now appeared it might endanger Mrs. Romero's house.

Father Ronquillo's none too subtle barb at Frank Del Roble had left the reporter muttering under his breath. "Superstitious fools, that's what," he reiterated to himself.

Frank's dream was to someday work for the *Los Angeles Times*, a newspaper of record with an enormous readership that Frank considered worthier of his considerable journalistic talents than the few thousand readers of the *Arroyo Daily News*. Frank believed that his strict adherence to scientific truth was his ticket to the big time.

As if to prove to himself and those around him that he was not in the least bit superstitious, he challenged in a voice loud enough for everyone in the crowd around him to hear, "If this is a miracle, may the earth open up and swallow me!"

No sooner had the words left his mouth, then a deep reverberation began in the ground immediately underneath Frank. The journalist's face blanched white as the whole area around Mrs. Romero's front yard began to tremble and rock, knocking several people off their feet and forcing everyone to struggle for balance.

Don Sabastiano, who in his many travels had experienced more than his share of life's wonders, immediately called out a warning to his neighbors. "Hold on to something, it's an earthquake!"

But an earthquake it was not. For just as quickly as it had started, the shaking subsided and was replaced by a loud rumbling sound rolling from under the sinkhole. While Frank caught his breath, reassured that the ground on which he stood was firm, the attention of the crowd was focused on the sinkhole as water began spouting up into the air.

The rolling rumble grew to a crescendo. When the noise had risen to a level that caused people to hold their hands over their ears, the sinkhole emitted a deafening whoosh.

With a power that sent water spraying a hundred yards in all directions, the sinkhole suddenly belched up the full frame of a 1949 black Chevy Fleetline.

O O O

"Get the hook around the front bumper," seventeen-year-old Pete Navarro called out as he stuck his head out of the cab of his Uncle Mickey's tow truck. It was four o'clock in the afternoon, an hour after the appearance of the 1949 Chevy Fleetline.

Rudy Vargas, Pete Navarro, David Sandoval, 'Lil Louie Ruiz, and Arroyo Grande, teenagers whose reputations were murky but who never actually been caught doing anything illegal, had agreed to haul the car out of Mrs. Romero's yard as a favor to *la señora* and for whatever parts they might strip from the vehicle.

As they prepared to haul the car, which looked like a giant bloated cockroach, out of the sinkhole, they discovered to their surprise that it was in remarkably good shape for having been completely submerged in water for who knows how long.

"Look," said Rudy, sitting atop the roof of the car still floating in the middle of the sinkhole, "it's a little rusty, but this chrome can be polished up." The steady bubbling of water from under the sinkhole seemed to keep the car afloat.

"We give it a new paint job," he continued, "replace the engine, some new upholstery, and this could be quite a nice ride."

"Doesn't look like it was in the water very long at all," 'Lil Louie agreed, sipping a coke as he sat on Mrs. Romero's porch. Somehow when Rudy, Pete, David, and Louie undertook enterprises, it was always Rudy, Pete and David who wound up doing the work, and Louie who managed to oversee the operation. "My managerial talents at work," he would explain.

The neighbors of Arroyo Grande gawked in wonder at the durable automobile defying the laws of nature by floating on the surface of the sinkhole. The water line went up to the car wheels.

"All set?" Pete cried out.

"*¡Dale!*" Rudy replied.

With a lurch, Pete began to edge the tow truck away from the sinkhole, slowly turning the car on its axis in the water and bringing it up to the shore of what could now be properly called the pond in Mrs. Romero's front yard.

The crowd watched with anticipation as the cable on the tow truck lifted the front end of the Fleetline out of the water. "Let me get off," yelled Rudy as he jumped off the hood of the car.

Pete waited until Rudy was clear and then continued to lift the car out of the water and over the sidewalk. But then the lifting stopped.

The tow truck alone could not get the Chevy's back wheels onto the sidewalk where Mrs. Romero's white picket fence had been. The car's upper end was in the air and its bottom end in the sinkhole.

"Come on guys," said Rudy to the men in the crowd, "*pasa mano.*"

Miguelito Pérez, Rudy Vargas, David Sandoval, Frank Del Roble, and Lil Louie gathered themselves under the car and began to push extra hard from below as Pete tried the lift again. Slowly the Chevy's rear end rose out of the water. The men shoved some more, each one straining to the limit of his strength.

Finally, the car's rear wheels touched the sidewalk.

It was a dramatic moment and the crowd could not help but give out a collective "Ah" as the back wheels of the vehicle caught hold of the ground. Within seconds

Pete was driving the tow truck down the street, dragging the dripping Chevy behind it.

"*¡Gracias a Dios!*" Mrs. Romero said. "I don't know how I would have gotten that thing out of there. You boys, *son tan buenos muchachos.*"

As the commotion of the Chevy Fleetline's departure quieted down, Choo Choo Torres noticed something along the edge of the sinkhole's water line.

He called Frank Del Roble over and the two conferred in whispers for a moment. Frank took a stick and held it against the side of the hole for a moment and then nodded to Choo Choo that he was right. Choo Choo turned to the crowd and announced loudly, "Mrs. Romero. Look! The water's going away."

Mrs. Romero and her neighbors gathered at the edge of the pond and saw that, sure enough, like the water in a sink when the plug is pulled, the water in her sinkhole seemed to be receding slowly into the depths of the earth.

The Chevy Fleetline had been the last item to come out of the sinkhole, and now it seemed as if some master magician had decided that the show was over and it was time to go home.

Indeed, with the sun now low in the sky, people began to remember those things they had set out to do on that Saturday before the commotion at Mrs. Romero's had distracted them—the shopping, the wash, the mowing of the lawn, the repairs around the house. One by one, Mrs. Romero's neighbors began to drift away.

"*Adiós, Señora Romero,*" said Mrs. Domínguez as she and her friends Sally and Doña Cuca left the sinkhole. They each carried something from the sinkhole: Mrs. Domínguez, a fake pearl broach and a bright red umbrella; Sally, a yellow and brown umbrella and a pair of harlequin style sunglasses; and Doña Cuca, a set of ceramic wind chimes and a book of *adivinanzas.* They were joined by Bobby Lee Verdugo, who had picked up a shiny brass tuba, and his wife Yolanda who had picked up an old issue of Life magazine and a tambourine. A noisy and colorful spectacle they all made walking up *Calle Cuatro* together, Bobby blowing notes on the tuba, Doña Cuca tapping the wind chimes, and Yolanda banging the tambourine in time to the music.

"*Sí, hasta luego*," said Juan Alaniz, flipping the silver dollar he had picked up earlier. Eugenia, his wife, carried off a pile of shirts and a bag of shoes. "For the homeless," she had explained earlier. "I'll drop them by the Goodwill on Monday."

Fearful that she would have to call a trash man to haul away what remained of the collection of artifacts, Mrs. Romero urged her neighbors to take what they wanted home. "*¡Llévenselo todo!* she said, "take anything you want!"

Don Sabastiano complied by carting off a sturdy wooden push broom with a wide bristle head.

Ed Carillo took a couple of old magazines that caught his eye. Thirty-five year old spinster Rosalinda Rodríguez took a white terry-cloth robe with her initials on it. The robe fit her perfectly, which was surprising since the poor woman was constantly ridiculed for being the most overweight person in Arroyo Grande.

Don Carlos Vasquez, who owned the Copa de Oro bar as well as several empty lots in Arroyo Grande, took a deck of Hoyle playing cards and a ring of assorted keys.

Twenty-two year old Julia Miranda, a dark-haired beauty who had been voted most likely to succeed by her high-school graduating class, and whose ambition was to someday star in a Hollywood movie, took an autographed photo of Carmen Miranda, a pair of sunglasses and a New York subway token.

No one really took note of who took what from the sinkhole—except perhaps when seven-year-old Moisés Armenta walked up to his mother with an unopened package of condoms.

With the adults in the crowd chuckling, Mrs. Armenta quickly took the condoms from the child and put them in her purse where they remained for several weeks until discovered by her husband Arnulfo when he was rifling through her purse looking for cigarette money.

By six that evening, when the street lamps began to go on up and down *Calle Cuatro*, all the items but an orange dog food dish, a yellow flyswatter and the Pérez Prado album had been taken away.

It was then that Mrs. Romero remembered that the whole day had started with her going into the back yard to feed Junior, and that in the course of the day's confusion she had forgotten to do that.

She looked out at her watery front yard, lit up by the street lights, and considered herself lucky.

The accidental appearance of the sinkhole had disrupted the mundane pattern of her daily activities and had given her a new appreciation for life. She wasn't sure what, if anything, it had done for her neighbors— but what a nice day it had turned out to be for her! Mrs. Romero was not an overly philosophical person, but as she stood on her porch watching the evening wrap itself around the modest houses of *Calle Cuatro*, she did have to wonder about the day's events.

Perhaps it was the mysterious workings of God, as Father Ronquillo had suggested. Or perhaps it was some other playful, magical force that had nudged her life and that of her neighbors. Or perhaps it was simply the overflow of the Rio Grande through a junk yard, all of it quite explainable by science.

Whatever the case, she was tired of thinking about it and eager to get on with the Pedro Infante movie, *Nosotros los pobres*, scheduled for TV that night. "Come on, Junior," she said, picking up the food dish, the flyswatter, and the album. "*Pobrecito*, it's time we got you some breakfast."

Last Night
of the Mariachi

Last Night of the Mariachi

The large silver coin emitted a high-pitched whine as it spun erratically, like a drunken top, on the mahogany counter at the Copa de Oro. As it spun about, reflecting the bar's neon beer signs in a sparkling array of yellow, red and blue, it hit a wine glass and then a mug half-filled with beer. This set off harmonic reverberations in the glassware and, together with the coin's own sound, completed perfectly the three notes of an A chord. Finally, it came to a rest just short of going over the counter edge, collapsing like an exhausted musician at the end of a premiere solo performance.

I picked it up and spun it again. As I played with the shiny silver dollar that had come bubbling up from the clear waters of Mrs. Romero's sinkhole several days before, I took another swallow of my second tequila of the night.

I usually don't drink much, not while working anyway. Some people will tell you that drinking makes a musician play better. That it makes you looser, more relaxed. Well, that may work for some *músicos*, but it doesn't work for me. When I play, I need to be sober. I'll be truthful, it's the only way I can follow the rest of the boys.

But tonight I had a special reason for drinking. I had to find some courage real fast. Don Carlos had asked me to go up to his office during our first break of the evening. I knew that he was going to hit us with something.

It was Tuesday night. Usually Tuesdays are pretty good at the Copa de Oro. Hell, I've seen the place packed with fifty, even sixty people—so many that Miguelito couldn't set them up fast enough. But tonight was different. It was very slow, only one of several slow Tuesday nights we'd been having since the Arriba opened up down the street. Here it was, after the second set, close to 10 PM, and still only eight people in the place! *¡Qué caray!*

The Arriba had opened up a couple of months before, and at first we really hadn't thought much of it— restaurants and bars come and go in the barrio with the frequency of arrests.

"They'll be out of business in a month," I'd told Fariño Gómez, the trumpet player of our group. "We've had competition before. And we've survived. Why? Because the Copa has something none of these new places have. It's got history; it's got tradition. Aren't we the only mariachi in the barrio that goes back thirty-two years? Aren't we the best?" Fariño was all too happy to agree.

And we were—until the Arriba.

The scheme of a southwest businessman, the idea behind the Arriba was to go into barrios from Tucson to Brownsville with a chain of trendy Mexican restaurants aimed at the younger set.

They had a mariachi, to be sure, but only Friday nights and for Sunday brunch, and one that knew how to cater to American as well as Mexican clientele. The mainstay was a disc jockey playing disco and rap music on week nights, and a live rock-and-roll band on Saturdays. Experience a bit of old Mexico with a modern touch! Well, maybe it'd work in San Antonio or Tucson, but we didn't figure it had a chance in Arroyo Grande. Or so we thought.

Within a couple of weeks of the Arriba's grand opening, we began to see the effect on the Wednesday night crowd. Old-timers who'd been with us for years said they were going to visit, just for one night, *"No más 'pa ver que hay.*" Then, the Thursday night crowd began to taper off. After another week, the Arriba was cutting into our weekend crowd—and the regulars hadn't returned. It was then that Don Carlos began to get worried.

I gulped a third tequila as I moved off the bar stool, pocketed the silver dollar, and started up to Don Carlos's office above the kitchen. "Might as well find out what's eating him," I said, loud enough for Miguelito to hear. Mixing a drink behind the counter, Miguelito nodded a "good luck" to me.

As I walked up the stairs, the silver dollar jingled in my pocket against my car keys. How many times had I been up these same steps? I remembered when the burgundy carpeting had just been installed, snug and form-fitted to the steps. It was a pleasure just to run your fingers through the thick pile. The burgundy had long ago faded to brown and now the carpeting was so worn that the wooden steps showed through what little of the carpet remained.

I thought about the many times I had gone up to the office. The first time was when Don Carlos had given us our "break" over thirty-two years ago. We'd been pretty green then, asking only for a chance to moonlight in order to make ends meet. Young *chavos*, fresh with the energy of musicians waiting for the big break, we were all too eager to play to an audience, no matter how small, and for whatever he'd pay us, no matter how little.

Later, when we were packing them in, we thought we deserved a raise for the midnight set. Up the stairs I had gone, as the leader of our group, and, hell, Don Carlos had been fair about it. And another time, when Braulio Armendáriz, who played violin, had been in a car accident, without even being asked, Don Carlos had advanced his family a loan. Or the time Pablo Figueroa, who played lead guitar in the group and occasionally doubled on trumpet, needed a new set of teeth, Don Car-

los had come through then as well. So, once again, up
those stairs.

"*Siéntate*, Juan," Don Carlos said, motioning to a
chair. I sat down opposite his desk, covered with
receipts and invoices. Don Carlos believed in doing his
own bookkeeping. He pushed aside what looked like
contracts and looked seriously at me for several
moments. I was on guard. Usually, he was not so formal
or serious.

"*Mira*," he said, settling back in his naugahyde arm-
chair. "There are some things that have happened that I
need to talk to you about. The boys...well, you can
explain it to them later. It's about the Arriba down the
street. It's taking a lot of our business. And do you know
why?"

I shook my head no, pretending I was born yesterday. Hell, let him play it the way he wanted it. Why I
should I help? He folded his hands over his ample stomach and shook his head as if lecturing an errant school-
boy.

"Because the Arriba is with the times, Juanito.
They're with the times! They have a new disco, they
have flashing lights, they have cocktail waitresses with
the little skirts that go all the way up to their *nalgas*.
They're with it, Juanito, that's what the public wants!"

I knew the rest of what he would say even before he
said it. The part about "I love you guys like my own
brothers, you know that. And I've always respected your
music..." And then the part about "but we have to keep
up with the times or else we'll go out of business..." And
lastly, when he was really fired up and had convinced
himself that firing us was in all our best interests, the
line about "it's really for your own good."

"Look at you," he said. "You're all past sixty-five!
Hombre, you should have retired long ago. This is not an
old man's sport, you know!" That's the one that hurt the
most of all. *¡Caray!*

By the time he was finished there was little I could
say on behalf of myself or the others except that we
would like to play out the week to Saturday.

"Sure, *hombre*," he said. "Sure! I was planning on it!
Play out the week and invite your friends. We'll make a
party of it. And if you need a letter or anything, *tú sabes*,
if you want to play someplace else, you can count on
me."

Back downstairs the group was preparing for the
next set. Fariño was doing lip warm-ups on the trumpet.
Cha Cha Mendiola was strapping on his *guitarrón*.
Braulio and Pablo were tuning up their strings. Cha
Cha gave me a questioning look—but I ignored it. "*¿Lis-
tos?*" I asked. They nodded. "Then let's get started." The
bad news could wait.

○ ○ ○

The rest of the evening went slowly. We began the
third set with the usual opening of *La Negra*, then we
went into our medley of mariachi favorites,
Guadalajara, *Soy Puro Mexicano*, *El Carretero*, *Camino
Real De Colima* and *Corrido de Chihuahua*.

"*...Qué lejos estoy del suelo donde he nacido...*"

We finished up the evening with *Canción Mixteca*.
By then some of our old friends had arrived: Kiki
Sánchez, who had once bought drinks for the house
when we played him *Las Mañanitas* on his birthday;
and the Maldonado brothers who ran the garage across
the street; and Chato Pastoral who never seemed to
have a job but always had money enough for his *tragos*;
and the others—Lefty Ramírez who, despite his age,
still hoped to play in the major leagues someday; one-
eyed Juan Lara; and Don Sabastiano, the Spaniard who
had fought in the Spanish Civil War.

We closed early that night. I collected a pitiful
$12.35 from the cracked fish bowl that Fariño had found
one summer in a trash can and on which he had later

painted the word "TIPS." I called the boys together in the parking lot and broke the news to them.

"What do you mean, let us go?" said Pablo, blinking in disbelief. "We've been playing at the Copa for thirty-two years! Doesn't that mean anything to Don Carlos? *¡Qué ingrato!*"

"I told him all of that," I said, "but it doesn't matter. 'Business is business,' he says, and we have to see his point of view. Don Carlos has been good to us, but he'll go out of business if things keep up this way."

"Well, it's not our fault," joined in Cha Cha, leaning on his *guitarrón*, whose shape had a striking similarity to his body. "If the Arriba is stealing away our customers, it's because they have better food and good-looking waitresses. Don Carlos should get a new cook and get some *viejas* into this place. That's what I think!"

"*¡Cállate!*" I warned, motioning to where Alfredo, the Copa's cook of ten years, was getting into his primer-spotted station wagon. "It's not just the food or the women. Things are changing. Music is changing. People's tastes are changing. They just don't like our kind of music anymore. They're tired of it."

"They've never been tired before," said Braulio. "Why now?"

"Don't take it personal, Braulio," I said. "It's the younger generation, *¿sabes?* They don't listen to mariachis anymore. It's all electronic now. *Rockenrollers*, you know."

"So, now what?" asked Fariño.

We were all silent for some time, each of us was thinking about what the answer might be. After thirty-two years in the same place, we knew we had nowhere else to go. We had gotten used to playing the old favorites at the Copa. The *rancheras* on Wednesdays and Thursdays, the love ballads on Fridays when the men came in lonely, wanting to drink to sad songs. We had even gotten used to pleasing the *gringo* tourists with countless repeat performances of *La Bamba*.

But the sad truth was that we hadn't learned a new song since the regulars nearly rioted and forced us to learn *Volver, Volver*. What did we have? Five *veteranos* whose dreams of playing in the big night clubs of our youth had long ago vanished into the day-to-day of buying shoes for the kids, tires for the car, and covering the month's rent. We were five guys who played each night, if only to remind ourselves that some part of that dream still lived in each of us. A sad lot now, with a violin that was perpetually out of tune, a cracked fish bowl that seldom saw tips, and no new songs to sing.

It was no wonder that Don Carlos was throwing us out—the surprising thing was that he had waited this long.

"We'll play out the week," Fariño said. "What else can we do?" We all nodded in agreement.

"But we can still make this the best week yet," I said. "We can play so good they'll never forget us!" I said it with more gusto than I had intended or thought I had in me, but it seemed to catch on.

"That's exactly what we'll do," Cha Cha agreed. "We'll show these *cabrones*!"

It was good to see our spirits back. We called it a night. I gave Braulio a ride home—his pick-up was in the shop again. Then I went home myself. Thirty-two years.

○ ○ ○

The next night we all showed up early and I thought that maybe our positive attitude would turn things around. By 8:30 we had twenty people in the bar. Not bad at all for a Wednesday night. But by the second set we were down to an even dozen, and nobody was buying food, just stringing out each drink. Don Carlos hated that. He told Alfredo to go home. We closed early again, before eleven, with only $6.50 in the fishbowl. It was embarrassing. I bought a round of drinks for the boys and we sat around and talked with Miguelito, who was cleaning up behind the counter.

"Don't worry, *muchachos*," he said, "when things get better, I'll speak to Don Carlos myself and have him bring you back." That was Miguelito for you, always promising things he could never deliver.

"Sure, it's just a temporary thing," said Cha Cha, already drunk and slurring his words. "You'll see. It's just a temporary thing."

Thursday was a bit better. We got in a crowd of *gringo* college students bar-hopping the barrio. They didn't get much further than the Copa; they really liked our music. I didn't know whether to appreciate it or feel offended.

Our own friends were deserting us and the only ones who seemed to like our music were outsiders. We played *La Bamba* and *La Paloma* two times each for them and they left us a hefty $25.00 tip. We ended with a total of $36.40 for the evening. When we split it up, it wasn't a whole lot for any of us, but at least I had something else to jingle in my pocket with the silver dollar that I now carried as a good-luck piece.

Friday was a disaster. Pablo called in sick and Braulio said his pick-up had broken down again and he was going to work on it that night at the Maldonado Brothers' garage. Fariño, Cha Cha, and I sat around for an hour before we decided to play a modified set with me covering lead guitar and Fariño the violin. We played the first set to a table of six people who ignored us totally. Half-way through my introduction to our favorite medley, the group got up and left. I finished the introduction to Cha Cha, Fariño, and Miguelito behind the bar. Don Carlos walked in about then, saw what had happened, and told us to call it a night.

We gathered around the bar and Miguelito served us each a beer, "On the house." We drank in silence, each of us hurting inside. Hurting because our good friend and *cuate* Don Carlos had put us out to pasture.

Hurting because we knew we couldn't compare with the discos and the *rockenrollers*. Hurting, most of all, because each of us knew we were the last.

Braulio, who was older than the rest of us, had actually played back-up mariachi for Pedro Infante in the early 50's—before Infante's tragic death. Pablo had learned his *requinto* from the Taríacuri. I had learned *segunda* and a little lead guitar getting drunk over my first love, lost to the sounds of José Alfredo Jiménez and Cuco Sánchez and Don Pedro's *Tecatitlán*. And now we were the last.

"We're going to miss you, Juanito." It was Raúl Maldonado. He and Don Sabastiano had come in and joined us at the bar. As Miguelito poured them drinks, Raúl limped over to me and put his hand on my shoulder. He walked with a limp because of the three toes he had left behind in Germany during World War II. "You know, there'll never be a mariachi like you boys."

"*The just man walketh in his integrity*. Proverbs Twenty, Seven," said Don Sabastiano as he took a seat next to Cha Cha.

Cha Cha, who was getting into one of his mean, drunken moods on the one beer alone, started to complain. "We wouldn't have to leave if there was more support from the *cabrones* who live around here! Instead, they go for the *gringo* music."

The sounds from the Arriba were in fact louder now, filtering through the door as if to underscore Cha Cha's point.

Don Sabastiano sipped on his beer and turned to Cha Cha. "*To everything there is a season*," he offered, "*and a time to every purpose under heaven*. Ecclesiastes Three, One."

"*¡Vete mucho a la chingada!*" Cha Cha replied, in no mood for Don Sabatiano's philosophizing.

"*¡No se hagan!*" Don Sabastiano insisted. "You all know its time for you to quit. *Mira*, I've been around for a while, and, believe me, I've seen life come and go. I think its time you fellows sit this one out. *Y no se hagan de chiple*. Let the younger generation have their day in the sun."

"Turn on your friends, eh, Don Sabastiano?" Cha Cha was really feeling his drink now. "Listen to that noise. Do you call that music? That's the noise my electric toaster makes in the morning. And worse, they dance to it!"

Don Sabastiano was not to be put off. "Can't you see that there is a time for everything—like it says in the *Santa Biblia*? *Hombre*, you had your turn. Don't you think thirty-two years is enough? You can't complain. Now, step aside and let others have their fun. I understand this new band that's coming in…"

Don Sabastiano instantly knew he had made the mistake of his life. We all turned to him as one.

"What new band?"

Don Sabastiano averted his eyes and turned to stare moodily into his beer. He was silent.

"Tell us!" I demanded, feeling my face flush with anger.

From behind us the unmistakable voice of Don Carlos answered back. "I'll tell you," he said, coming over and putting one hand on Cha Cha's shoulder and the other on mine. "Since it seems some people can't keep their mouths shut." He glared at Don Sabastiano for a moment, then turned to us.

"Boys, I've hired a new band. They'll be coming in on Sunday. They're a younger group, play modern stuff and some traditional, and on weekends they can play rock and roll for the younger *gente*. Don't take this personal, boys, I just have to do it."

I shrugged his hand off my shoulder and turned to Cha Cha, wondering if he would go for Don Carlos's throat the way he had once when he thought Don Carlos had cheated us out of a week's pay. But the news was even too much for Cha Cha. He took another swallow and was silent.

Don Carlos was going through his own hell, I could see, although it didn't make me feel any better. He stood there, embarrassed, looking to Miguelito for support.

"They're called the Diablos del Eastside," he said finally. And then, as an afterthought, as if it would make things any better, "They're just young kids..."

I motioned to the boys. Fariño nodded and began to collect his trumpet. I helped Cha Cha with the *guitarrón*. Outside we walked slowly to the cars, none of us saying much. Across the street I could see that the light at Maldonados was still on—Braulio was still at it. I knew what we were thinking. What was the use of coming back tomorrow? To go through more humiliations? To have another group of tourists walk out on us?

As we passed the billboard outside the Copa, I stopped and looked up at the aged marquee which announced in letters that had long ago merged with the gray dirt of the marquee:

LIVE ENTERTAINMENT
LAS NUEVAS CALAVERAS
TUESDAY THROUGH SATURDAY

Fariño and Cha Cha stopped by my side. We stayed there for a while, just staring up at the sign, not saying anything. Finally Cha Cha picked up his *guitarrón*, "I'll see you guys tomorrow. I'm going to play even if there's only Miguelito there to listen!" We all knew it, but Cha Cha had made it public—we had a tradition to maintain and we would play it out to the end.

○ ○ ○

By nine o'clock the next morning I had turned in my faded *charro* outfit at the cleaners. I paid extra so they would have it ready by mid-afternoon. After that, I went over to Portello's Music Shop and got a new set of strings for my guitar—just in case. I worked the rest of the morning at resetting the three pieces of ivory inlay that had fallen out of the fretboard years ago.

By three, my *charro* suit was ready. We had long ago given up playing in full *charro* dress each night. Dry cleaning made it too expensive. Over the years we had given up entirely, but tonight would be something special. At least for me.

Eugenia, bless her, had polished my boots by the time I got back from the cleaners. She had been really considerate since I had told her the bad news. With Michael and María grown and married, she knew how much my playing meant to me. She helped me mend the two missing buttons on my jacket. As I walked to the car, she surprised me by pinning to my lapel a small carnation that she had cut from the garden. She secured it with an elegantly crafted silver pin that she had picked up from Mrs. Romero's sinkhole the week before. *¡Caray!* What a woman!

I arrived at the Copa to warm up an hour before we usually met. The rest of the band was already there. I slid into the long booth with the stuffing coming out of the seats. For years it had been our home base. Miguelito brought me over a beer as I looked from Pablo to Braulio to Fariño and to Cha Cha. They were each wearing *their* charro suits.

"It must be—how do you call it when you speak with your mind?" Fariño asked with a smile.

"Telepathy," I told him.

He held up his beer. "*Pues*, to telepathy, then, *muchachos!*"

We drank it down.

We began to talk, to laugh, to remember. We drank for an hour, remembering old friends who over the years had enjoyed our music but who were now gone. We recalled the night Chuy Madrigal came in drunk and had challenged everyone in the house to a fight and then fell flat on his face asleep before anyone could reply. Another time, before Johnny Ríos got picked up for drugs, he had challenged Don Carlos to a tequila-drinking bout. Miguelito had served tequila shots to Johnny but only plain water to Don Carlos for half an hour before Johnny caught on. There was also the time we had volunteered a Mother's Day medley to a sad woman drinking by herself, only to discover later that she *was* a mother, but that her only son was in the *torcida*, doing life without parole.

By 6:30 there was still no one in the bar but us and Miguelito. Don Carlos had sent Alfredo home and had gone upstairs to work on the books. It didn't look good.

At 7:00 Miguelito asked us to watch the bar while he went out to get supplies down the street. With the affair he was carrying on with young Julia Miranda, who lived nearby on Tenth Street, I could well imagine what supplies he was getting. When 7:30 came and there were still no customers, we decided to warm up anyway.

Over the years we had become bored with warm-ups. We had gotten to the point where we would just tune up before the set and immediately jump into a well-known favorite like *La Negra* or *El Carretero*. But tonight was different. We spent time tuning and retuning our instruments so that when Pablo checked his guitar with the tuning fork, it set up vibrations in the *guitarrón* and the violin as well.

> *"Nadie comprende lo que sufro yo,*
> *Canto porque no puedo sollozar..."*

We began with *Perfidia*, Braulio's clear voice reaching into the rafters of the darkened bar. We played slowly, rhythmically. Fariño's telepathy must have been working again, because with just a nod of my head we slid into a medley of *boleros: Sin Ti, Perdón*, and *Sabor a Mí*. By the time we were ready for more upbeat standards, we had left the bar behind us and were playing to ourselves. For ourselves.

After an hour, Braulio noticed that Miguelito had
not returned. Braulio went over to the bar and got us
another round of beers. On his way back, he closed the
door that was letting in the disco sounds from the
Arriba. We began another set.

This time it was a potpourri of *corridos* from the
Revolution. We had learned many of these songs as children and knew them as well as we knew our own
names.

> "*Carabina, treinta-treinta,*
> *que los Villistas portaban...*"

Our sound was now more intoxicating to us than the
beer. As Braulio and I took turns on the verses of *Corrido de Cananea*, *Valentín de la Sierra*, and *Siete
Leguas*, we drank in, deep and full, each sustained note,
each *ajúa*, each *grito*.

> "*Siete Leguas el caballo,*
> *que Villa más estimaba...*"

As we finished up the *corridos*, Pablo nodded to me
and pointed with his chin at two men who were seated
in the shadows of one of the back booths. I couldn't
make them out very well, but they seemed to be enjoy-
ing the music. Hell, we had an audience after all.

"*¡Bienvenidos!*" I shouted at them. They smiled and
waved back at me. Even in the darkened bar, one of the
men looked familiar, but I couldn't quite place the mustache and strong Indian features. There was something
about his hat—that's what it was! I hadn't seen a hat
like that since the early fifties.

Next, we went into songs that we had not sung for
years. Songs that were old when we learned them as
teenagers, songs whose lyrics we miraculously remembered after having forgotten them for decades.

> "*...de dos hermanos muy buenos,*
> *que tuvieron que pelear...*"

The more we played, the more inspired we became. Our music was flowing smoothly, like crystal sap from a cut *maguey*. It was then I noticed that several more people had entered and taken seats, anonymous silhouettes that settled comfortably amid the back shadows of the bar. We finished up the "oldies" set with *Me Voy pa'l Pueblo* and received wild applause from a room that was now filled with about twenty people.

As I started in on the patter introducing our next set of songs, I saw that there was something different about this crowd. I didn't recognize any of our regulars, and yet some of these faces—they seemed so familiar. There were handsome men here, and beautiful women. Some were dressed strangely, in the old-fashioned garb of years gone by. Others that I could see more closely appeared dressed in suits of the forties: here and there I could make out a pair of shiny *calcos*; over there a slick *tando*; and more than one swinging gold chain.

At another table, a group of *charros* sat, with eloquent sombreros that hid their faces but not their voices as they sang along with us. A costume party, I thought. That must be it. That's why they all seemed to know each other.

> "...se empieza siempre llorando,
> y así llorando se acaba..."

When we began an homage to José Alfredo Jiménez with *Camino de Guanajuato*, the audience erupted in applause.

This was our night to sing and they were really with us. They waved us on with *bravos* and *vivas*, whistles and handclaps. We sang of loves won and loves lost, of deceitful women and treacherous men, of the pain of loving and the joy of living, the melancholy of loves remembered and the promise of loves to be.

We sang about drunken *borracheras*, about lost sons, about courageous *revolucionarios* and daring *Adelitas*. We sang of needless tragedies, of dope deals gone wrong, of ungrateful women and brothers who fought. It was the lifeline of our people and as we tapped into it, we brought to life the hurts and joys of each song. Our audience loved it. They sang with us, and they clapped and shouted and cried.

As it got later and I could see the faces of that roaring audience better, I thought I did recognize a face here and there. But I knew I must be mistaken, for the names that came to mind were those of friends long dead, or of singers faintly remembered from my childhood, or of legendary greats long dead even before I was born.

In a back booth was the handsome *charro* with the thin black mustache and oversized hat. At another table sat a heavyset man with a shock of gray cutting through his otherwise black hair. And at another table there was a striking older gentleman, lean, distinguished, with the long fingers of a pianist. We sang, we sang, and still we sang.

> "...Mañana, me voy mañana,
> mañana, me voy de aquí..."

Until four in the morning. And then we stopped.

As we finished up the last verse of *El Quelite*, I looked once again out to the audience and found the room was empty. Not even Miguelito had returned.

"*Qué raro.*"

We looked at each other puzzled. "What happened to them?" asked Fariño. No, it hadn't been just my imagination.

"They must have left pretty fast," said Pablo. "I didn't even notice them leave."

"They didn't make much noise, either," said Fariño.

We looked around the room. There were no drinks on the tables, no dirty ashtrays, no emptied chip dishes. Yet only a few minutes before, the place had been packed. The smoke had cleared away, too, just like that.

"Wait a minute," said Fariño, very much troubled. "Did you notice those two guys over at the far booth? Didn't one of them look like..."

"Yes, yes!" interrupted Braulio. "Jorge Negrete! I'd know him anywhere. It was Jorge, I tell you, him in the flesh! I'll never forget that smile."

That put a chill up my spine and shut us all up for a long moment.

"¿Brujos?" I said. "You guys want me to believe in ghosts now?"

"It's true, Juanito," said Cha Cha excitedly. "I swear I saw the Trío Tariácuri, the originals, sitting over there to my left—que en paz descansen. And over at that table, that could only have been Don Augustín. Did you see him perk up when we played María Bonita? That woman with him, did you see them, just like love birds."

"Miguel Aceves! That was him right down here in the front row!" said Fariño. "And I'll bet my trompeta that was Guty Cárdenas there, surrounded by all those lovely ladies."

"Se acabó, muchachos," Pablo said. He wasn't buying any of this. "We're all tired and we've all had a little too much to drink."

"Pablo's right," I said, trying hard to convince myself that I believed it. "It's late, let's pack it up."

That broke the moment. Suddenly it was like every other night after closing. We began to pack up our instruments and clean up the playing area. While the boys collected our stuff outside the front door, I went upstairs to tell Don Carlos we were leaving. His office was empty. He must have gone home thinking Miguelito would lock up. I returned downstairs and turned off the barroom lights and made sure the windows were locked.

As I passed the broken fish bowl, I instinctively reached in. It was empty. I thought about it for a while. Outside I could hear the debate still going on. Pablo arguing that it was just some rude patrons who hadn't had the courtesy to say goodbye or leave a tip.

The others were convinced that we had been visited by the greats from the past.

I reached into my pocket and discovered among the nickels and dimes the silver dollar that had been jingling there all evening. I pulled it out and left it in the fishbowl. Tomorrow the new mariachi would be in, and even upstart young kids deserve a first tip.

An Unusual Malady

An Unusual Malady

The screen door slammed shut with a loud crash, sending a flurry of the door's weathered paint chips cascading down onto the wooden porch. A warm breeze swept across the porch just then, swirling the paint particles into a funnel that crept across the hardwood floor like a stylus, inking out a hidden message in paint and debris as it traveled over the worn crevices of the porch.

I struggled to balance the 1965 Smith Corona typewriter against my chest with one hand as I locked the screen-door latch behind me. It was the same typewriter that I'd rescued from Mrs. Romero's sinkhole the week before, and I was being very careful not to let it drop. I turned from the door and walked along the wooden porch that connected the three apartments in the long, barracks-like complex located at 301 Tenth Street. It had been my home for as long as I could remember.

The slats on the worn wooden porch creaked as I walked from our end of the building—where I lived with my mom and dad and sisters, María and Mónica—to the apartment at the other end which was occupied by Don Sabastiano Diamante and his ten-year-old dachshund Peanuts.

The third apartment, located between the other two, belonged to Julia Miranda, without question the most beautiful woman in the world. Slight, dark-haired, and twenty-two years old with large brown eyes that penetrated deep into your soul, she was my obsession and the one thing that made life bearable on Tenth Street. I had been in love with her for most of my twelve years, at least as far back as I could remember. I was convinced that someday I would marry her and spent most of my time fantasizing about what married life would be like with her.

She lived alone and, as was well known by just about everybody in Arroyo Grande, dreamed of someday starring in a Hollywood movie. Yoli Mendoza, who played second base on the Arroyo Grande Sluggers, made fun of her for this. I was always having to tell Yoli to shove it.

"You're just jealous 'cause you're not pretty enough to go to Hollywood and become a movie star," I'd say to her. Actually, Yoli wasn't so bad looking, except that she always dressed like us boys.

"At least I've got a brain," she'd reply.

Yoli didn't know that someday I would win Julia's love. None of my friends knew. It was my secret. They also didn't know that a week ago I had pulled out something from the waters in Mrs. Romero's front yard that was going to make Julia fall in love with me. It was a red and white packet of powder labeled *"Medicina de Amor."* With it and my Master Plan, I would win her love.

My Master Plan was the key to it all.

First, I'd become a great writer. Then, after my novels became best-sellers, Hollywood producers would want to make them into blockbuster movies. That's when I'd step in and intercede on her behalf.

I'd demand that Julia Miranda star in all of them. "It's Miranda or nothing!" I'd say. That is, if she wasn't already a star or, and this was my worse fear, married to the biggest weasel in Arroyo Grande, Miguelito Pérez. Spit in his face!

As I carried the typewriter past Julia Miranda's apartment window, I did what I always do when I pass her place.

I peeked in.

Once, last summer, I had gotten a glimpse of Julia's bare chest as she walked out of the shower stall with a towel wrapped around her waist. The momentary sight of her firm breasts and brown nipples was a delight that I had carried with me for weeks thereafter.

Each time I saw Julia hanging laundry in the back yard or coming home from the beauty salon where she worked, I would replay the sight of her naked breasts over and over again in my mind. What a sight!

Eventually, I had to stop doing that because she started looking at me funny. One afternoon she asked me if I was feeling okay and should I see a doctor. My face flushed and I got that sinking feeling in the pit of my stomach that I always get when I talk to her. I honestly get sick when I'm near her! I told her I was fine and quickly walked away. I didn't want to scare her off before I had a chance to put my Master Plan to work.

This time I caught Julia just as she had finished putting on her bra. My bad luck was with me as she chose that very moment to look up. She caught me staring at her. I remained transfixed.

I could feel my face growing hot with embarrassment, but I just couldn't take my eyes off her. She immediately walked to the window and closed the curtains in my face.

"¡Choo Choo Torres, I'm going to tell your mom!" she yelled through the paper-thin wall.

I moved on, cursing my bad luck for having arrived at the window a split second too late and for her having caught me. Damn! Now I'd have to make it up to her somehow. I sure hoped the love medicine would do the trick.

As I walked along the porch that linked the apartments together, I brushed against the wood slates of the apartment wall with my shirt sleeve, sending flakes of peeled yellow paint onto the porch. The building hadn't been painted in years. I was hoping I'd find Don Sabastiano Diamante at home. He's the greatest authority on

the Bible, the best fixer of broken things in Arroyo
Grande, a world traveler, and my special confidant.

When I got to his apartment, I knocked on the door
with my foot. There was no response. Then I heard Don
Sabastiano's voice booming from behind the barracks
structure, *"Therefore now amend your ways and your
doings, and obey the voice of the Lord your God.* Do it,
damn it!"

I sat the typewriter down on the porch and walked
down the steps and around the back where I found Don
Sabastiano and Peanuts in the empty field adjacent to
our apartment building. I watched from a distance. Don
Sabastiano carefully stalked a few feet behind Peanuts
as the dog went about its morning duties. The weiner
dog stopped to sniff at a clump of weeds, then carefully
walked around in a semicircle looking for just the right
place to deposit the remains of last night's dinner.

"Do it, Peanuts, do it!" Don Sabastiano said insis-
tently.

I joined Don Sabastiano as Peanuts bent his tubular
body into a hump, reminding me of a inch-worm I had
once found in a head of lettuce, and began the slow
process of dumping it all out. Those weiner dogs can
hold a lot!

"Good dog," said Don Sabastiano happily. As soon as
Peanuts was finished, Don Sabastiano picked up a stick
and started poking at the mound of excrement with
great urgency.

"Whacha' doing, Don Sabastiano?" I asked.

Don Sabastiano straightened up at the sight of me. I
think he was a bit embarrassed to be caught meddling
in his dog's doings.

"Ofelia's ring." He said cryptically.

He finished spreading the mess around the grass
and then, satisfied that he had not found what he was
looking for, let out a slow, emphatic "Damn!"

"Ofelia's ring?" I persisted.

"Ofelia's ring," Don Sabastiano reiterated sadly. He motioned for me to follow and headed back toward his apartment.

"Ofelia, may she rest in peace." Don Sabastiano explained as I caught up with him: "She gave me a gold wedding band in 1946, right after the war. I've worn it ever since." His voice was shaky, the way it got whenever he spoke of his wife who had died years ago.

Peanuts had run on ahead and was stopping every now and then to sniff at the tall grass that grew jungle-like around the apartment complex. Don Sabastiano had rheumatism, so we walked slowly back to the apartments.

"Last night, I took it off to wash paint from my hands and it dropped on the floor in the bathroom." Don Sabastiano continued. "Peanuts ate it!"

"Ohhhh," I said, looking at the dachshund, who looked back over its shoulder to me and waved its tail happily.

"The Lord giveth and the Lord taketh away," he said with a sigh. "Guess I'll have to take him to the vet."

We arrived at the steps in front of Don Sabastiano's apartment and he caught sight of the typewriter I'd left on the porch.

"Yours?" He asked.

I nodded, figuring now was the time to pitch the favor I needed.

"Don Sabastiano, this typewriter almost works, but some of the keys stick and I figured maybe you could fix it."

"Let me look at it," the old man said, sitting down on the porch and picking up the machine to examine it. He began to fiddle with this and that key and play with the bar mechanism that delivered the keys to the roller drum.

"What do you think? Can you fix it?" I asked.

"Looks like all it needs is a little cleaning," he said. "Some oil here and there and it should work fine."

"I need it for my office," I said.

"Office?"

"Yep," I explained proudly, "I'm opening up an office under the house here."

"Under the house?" Don Sabastiano asked, puzzled.

"Well, in the crawl space under the house. I'm going to have an office just like every good writer has."

I explained to him my Master Plan, at least the part about becoming a great writer, not about marrying Julia Miranda. The first step to becoming a great writer, I had decided months ago, was to open an office. All the writers I'd ever read about had offices, with a desk and a typewriter and lots of pencils. So that's what I needed: an office, a place where I could create!

When Mrs. Romero's sinkhole erupted last Saturday and items of all kinds began to bubble up into her front yard, I was quick to realize that there might be something there for me. I started pulling things out of the water and laying them on the sidewalk to dry. Pretty soon the other kids were helping me. As it turned out, there was a lot of great stuff that came up that day, and some of those objects fit neatly into my Master Plan.

That night I borrowed my sister Mónica's red Radio Flyer wagon and in it carried home four unopened gallon cans of semi-gloss paint primer, a 1965 Smith Corona typewriter, a pair of compasses, a ruler, five brand-new #2 pencils, a handful of ballpoint pens, a hardback copy of *David Copperfield*, a dictionary, and a stapler. A fine start start toward a well-equipped writer's office.

The other item I picked up at Mrs. Romero's was the packet of love medicine with a label showing a couple kissing and the inscription "win the heart of your true love."

○ ○ ○

"Well this is a malady for the books," the veterinarian chuckled. "I don't feel anything, but we can take some X-rays and see if something turns up."

It was several hours later and I had volunteered to accompany Don Sabastiano to the veterinarian's to see if they could locate the missing ring that Peanuts had swallowed. I figured it was the least I could do, since he had agreed to fix the typewriter.

We were gathered around a metal table in the center of a small examining room—Don Sabastiano, the vet, myself, and Peanuts. The vet had felt all under the dog's stomach and had looked down its throat, but had been unable to detect anything.

"You're sure he swallowed the ring?" the vet asked.

"Yes, oh yes," Don Sabastiano replied emphatically. "And I've checked his stool for a whole day now and *nada.*"

"Well, leave him overnight. We'll run some X-rays and check his stool here and see if we can come up with something."

"The X-rays will show anything there, right?" Don Sabastiano asked.

"Well, almost anything. Sometimes material in the intestinal track may occlude X-rays altogether. Some things dogs eat are impervious to X-rays. Take sponges for example, or baby-bottle nipples. If it's a ring, though, we should see it."

Don Sabastiano reluctantly agreed to leave Peanuts and said goodbye to the weiner dog, who was wagging his tail until he realized that he was not going home with the old man.

As we left the vet's office we could hear Peanuts' distinctive, high-pitched bark, rising in outrage above the din of the other dogs in the vet's kennel area.

"Useless mutt," Don Sabastiano said as we started the walk back home. "Don't know why I bother with it. If I don't find that ring, I'm going to put that dog to sleep. *Thou are weighed in the balance and are found*

wanting. Book of Daniel, Five, Twenty-seven. You mark
my words! That'll teach the little bastard!"

I didn't say anything. Most of the time Don Sabastiano talked like that, he didn't really mean it. Usually
it was after a stopover at the Copa de Oro, and people
will say anything after they've been *there* for an hour or
two. But once or twice he had actually carried out one of
his threats.

One time he swore he'd tear down the clothesline if
my mother continued to block his view of the Arroyo
Grande cemetery by hanging bed sheets outside his
apartment window. 'Amá thought he was exaggerating
until the day she had a particularly large batch of
clothes to hang and was busy at it when Don Sabastiano
suddenly came running out of his apartment.

He had a cold look in his eyes, one I had never seen
before. He walked up to my mother and said, "I meant
what I said," in a quiet, deliberate tone. He then proceeded to tear down all the lines from the two T-poles at
either end of the back yard, throwing all the wet clothes
on the ground. Boy, was 'Amá mad! Then Don Sabastiano just as calmly walked back into his apartment.

From then on 'Amá never blocked the view outside
his window again, you can bet on that!

For the sake of Peanuts, I figured it was best not to
try the old man's patience, so I didn't say anything
about him wanting to put the dog to sleep. We walked
home in silence.

In the afternoon I carefully placed a thin line of blue
powder in a semicircle around the front entrance to
Julia's apartment door. The instructions on the packet
said to do this and then speak to the person while he or
she was in the semicircle. They'd instantly fall in love
with you!

I waited on the steps outside Julia's apartment until
she came out on her way to Sally's Coiffers, where she
worked as a hair stylist. I quickly got up and gathered
my courage as she locked her apartment door. I hated

this! Every time I spoke to her it was the same thing: that sinking feeling deep in my gut, my face all hot and my hands all sweaty. I really felt sick. And then I'd forget to act cool, and usually made a fool of myself. But this time I was going to be in control.

"Miss Julia," I said, "I have something to say to you."

"What is it, you little escuincle?" she answered back harshly.

"I didn't mean to look into your window or to get you mad," I said. "It was an accident. And I certainly didn't mean you any disrespect. Julia, you know I respect you very much."

"Well, just make sure you don't do it again, Choo Choo." She lightened up a bit and smiled. "What's a handsome young guy like you doing looking into girl's windows, anyway? Don't you have a nice girlfriend someplace?"

I was dying inside. How could I tell her that *she* was the one I loved? That she was the woman I would some-day marry? I just played dumb and stalled for time. The packet didn't say how long you had to speak to the person inside the blue powder line. I hoped I was giving the magic powder enough time to work.

"Nah, I don't got much time for girls," I said. There was no way to keep her there anymore, so I started to back down the steps. "Uh, I gotta go to baseball practice now. Just didn't want there to be no hard feelings."

She smiled again. "No hard feelings here. And thank you very much for the apology. You're a real gentleman." With that she turned and walked away.

I stood there watching her walk down the walkway to Tenth Street. A gust of wind scattered the blue powder across the porch. Still, she had called me a real gentleman! Maybe the magic was working!

Late that night, I returned from the corner store where I had been sent by my mother to get bologna, bread, lettuce, and other fixings for my father's lunch the next day. As I passed by Don Sabastiano's apartment, I thought I heard noises coming from within.

I stopped for a moment to listen. At first I couldn't make out what the noise was, then I realized that what I was hearing was the old man crying, his breath going in and out in deep lonely sobs.

○ ○ ○

The next morning I got up early to apply the final coat of paint to the floor, walls, and desk of my office. I entered the crawl space through the ventilation screen behind the apartment and crawled to the area I had chosen for the office.

I had to be careful crawling around in the space under the house because the distance from the floorboards above and the bare earth was only three feet, and the space was haphazardly crisscrossed with pipes and electrical conduits.

Two days earlier, I had increased the headroom of my office area by digging out a large indentation in the bare earth, two feet deep and five feet by five feet square. I had cut a piece of used linoleum I'd picked up at the Goodwill thrift shop to fit into the floor and had jammed heavyweight cardboard along the four sides of the indentation to serve as walls.

An old wooden milk crate that I'd found in a back alley made an ideal desk for the typewriter. I used up all four of the cans of paint I'd recovered from Mrs. Romero's sinkhole to paint the floor, cardboard walls, and the desk. All in all, it was quite a neat and tidy affair, and I was quite proud of my ingenuity.

This morning, I worked quickly, hoping the final coat of paint would dry by the afternoon, when Don Sabastiano had promised he'd have the typewriter ready.

As I painted, I could hear my mother and father arguing above me. They had been arguing about something on and off for several days, but I didn't know exactly what it was. Every time I'd walk into the room they'd clam up and my mother would say to my father, "This isn't finished yet, Horacio."

I stopped my painting to see if I could figure out what it was they were arguing about, but then I heard my 'Apá say, "Anyway, I'll be late for work, but I still think you're being bull-headed about this, Refugia."

"¡Vete!" My mom said, "and if anyone is being bull-headed, it's you, Horacio. Who puts these ideas into your mind?" Then she shouted angrily. "¿Qué, estás loco? Don't you know there are laws?"

I heard my dad stomp out the apartment and slam the door behind him. I finished the painting and was about to go outside when I heard other voices reverberating through the ancient wood floors.

I crawled out of the office and started out on my hands and knees, stopping every now and then to make sure I was moving in the direction of the voices. Eventually, I found myself directly under Julia Miranda's apartment.

"Come on, Julia, you know you want it as much as I do."

The voice coming through the floorboards was pleading and earnest and belonged to Miguelito Pérez, the slimeball who worked at the Copa de Oro bar. He was Julia Miranda's steady boyfriend and my arch rival. Spit in his face!

"I told you, Miguelito, if you really love me, we can wait," I heard her say. "I have my career to think about."

I made myself comfortable in the space under the flooring and listened.

"Anyway," she continued, "you haven't answered my question. Do you think I look like her?"

"I don't know. Let me look at the photo again. Where'd you get this, anyway?"

"Mrs. Romero's."

"Hey, it's even autographed. 'With Love, Carmen Miranda.'"

"So, don't I look like her?"

"Yeah, I guess…"

"Miguelito, I think it's fate."

"That's what I've been saying, *cariño*. It's fate. This whole gigantic universe, and here you and I are together—it's a miracle! So why not give in to fate, *m'ija?*"

"That's not what I meant! It's fate that of all the things that came up from Mrs. Romero's sinkhole, I should pick up this photo. We have the same name, she was one of the only Latina movie stars, and now I find her photograph and it's autographed! It's a sign. It means I *am* going to be a movie star. Miguelito, stop that!"

"*Ay, cómo eres.* Come on Julia, don't be so stingy with your body. You *know* I really love you. You're my only girl. What more do you want?"

"I want to get out of Arroyo Grande, which I will do as soon as I save up enough money. And then I will go to Hollywood and get a job modeling. And eventually I will break into acting and become a star. But I can't do any of that if we do it and I get a swollen belly. *¿Me entiendes?*"

"We'll take precautions. You know me, *chula,* I am very careful! Come on over here, *mi chula.*"

This was not the first conversation I had overheard between Julia and weasel Pérez, and I didn't like them one bit. The weasel was always trying to stick his thing into Julia, but she wouldn't let him.

That's why I loved her.

She was being pure for the man she would marry, and that would be me. But she didn't know that yet. That is, if weasel Miguelito ever got out of the way. Spit in his face!

Most of the time the two spent talking mushy, the kind of stuff Julia and I would be talking after I became a famous writer and bought her a luxurious home in Beverly Hills. Sometimes they fought—that was the best! I was always hoping she'd give old pig-face the boot, but they always made up afterwards.

It was overhearing Julia and Miguelito that had first given me the idea to open my office under the apartments. The summer before I had been crawling under the house looking for the ground ball that Reymundo Salazar had hit through the ventilation door when I had heard voices and had traced them to Julia's apartment.

It occurred to me right there and then that, as a writer, I had the ideal opportunity to listen in on the lives of all the people who lived upstairs—my parents, my sisters, Julia and Miguelito, and Don Sabastiano—without them even knowing. What a great way to get material to write about!

That's when I had gotten the plan to open up my office right there under the house. That's where I'd listen, write, and prepare for the fame that would follow.

Julia and Miguelito's argument ended like it did other times, with a long period of silence. I figured she was probably letting him kiss her. That was okay by me, as long as she didn't *do it* with him or anyone else until I could marry her. I got bored and decided I'd better see Don Sabastiano about the typewriter.

I crawled out from under the house and went to see if Don Sabastiano was home, but he didn't answer my knocking. Then I remembered it was Thursday and that he was probably down at the cemetery.

I decided I'd go look for him and, sure enough, Don Sabastiano was on the hilly slope of the Arroyo Grande cemetery. He was surrounded by tombstones, leaning on a broomstick, looking very much like a human scarecrow protecting the dead. He was busily cleaning one of the flat, marble tombstones with the push broom that he had picked up from the sinkhole the week before. I didn't want to disturb him, so I just stayed down by the gate and watched from a distance.

He pushed the broad, bristled head of the push broom back and forth across the white-washed marble slab, sweeping dead mayflies, bird droppings, and dried leaves to the edge of the marble, over the side, and onto the cemetery grass. He worked methodically, patiently, as if he had all the time in the world. Now and then he'd get down on his hands and knees to scrub at a particularly difficult bit of dirt. His strokes were gentle and loving. Then he'd use the green rubber hose to wash the marble slab clean. Finally, when he finished, he stood back for a moment and leaned on the push broom to admire his work. The marble slab gleamed like a diamond in the afternoon sun. It was about three feet across and eight feet in length, and lay on the hilly incline of the cemetery.

I had seen it up close before and remembered it carried an inscription in neat, deep letters:

Ofelia Luisa Diamante
Beloved Wife
(1920-1978)

Lying side by side with the slab that Don Sabastiano had just cleaned was another marble slab, identical to the first except that it contained no inscription. I had asked him once about that and he had suddenly gotten very silent. Finally, he had turned to me and said, "*When this corruptible shall have put on incorruption and this mortal shall have put on immortality, then shall be brought to pass the saying that is written, Death is swallowed up in victory.* First Corinthians, Fifteen, Fifty-four."

I never asked him about it again.

Now, Don Sabastiano leaned over his wife's tombstone and spoke to her. "There you are, *m'ija*." He said aloud. "It's nice and clean for you." I was glad that I'd stayed out of sight. This was private. He finished washing off the marble slab with the hose and then began to work on the other tombstone.

For as long as I could remember, Don Sabastiano had come to the cemetery every other day. Sometimes he'd come in the early morning, sometimes, like today, in the late afternoon, but always it was the same. He washed his wife's tombstone first, then moved on to his own.

"*M'ija*, don't worry about it," he said, continuing his conversation out loud. "It'll turn up. That Dr. Richardson, he's a good vet. He knows what he's doing."

He got up off his knees and washed down the second marble slab with water. Satisfied with the morning's work, he collected the push broom, pail of soap and water, and the garden hose and stored them in the cemetery's tool shed. Then he returned to his wife's tombstone.

"I'm sorry about this *pendejada*," he said, looking down at the tombstone. He shifted his weight from one foot to another. I could tell his rheumatism was hurting him. "I'll make it up to you. Goodbye, *m'ija*, I'll be back tomorrow."

I waited until he was down the hill by the cement walkway that led to the main gate before I revealed myself. I made as if I had just now walked through the gate.

"Hi, Don Sabastiano. I came by to see if maybe you had fixed the typewriter."

"Hi, *m'ijo*," he said, smiling. I guess the visit to the cemetery had cheered him up. Anyway, he sure seemed more friendly than the last time I had seen him. "Yes, I got it back at the house. *¡Vamos!* Let's go get it for you."

We returned to his apartment and he handed me the typewriter. Boy, what an excellent job he had done! He had cleaned the drum and the letters, polished the return handle, and had even shined up the body with some kind of polish. It sparkled!

That afternoon I installed the typewriter in my office, setting it on top of the wood-crate desk. Next to it I placed an empty, clean *enchilada*-sauce can filled with pencils and pens I had accumulated in the past week. In the space under the typewriter I carefully stored the pair of compasses, ruler, stapler, the copy of *David Copperfield*, the *Webster's Dictionary,* and other office supplies I had found.

Outside the ventilation door I hung a piece of plywood four inches wide and fifteen inches across. I had painted it white and then had printed in large letters: C.C. Torres - Writer.

I now had my own office!

○ ○ ○

Peanuts returned the next day.

The vet had been unable to find anything, and once again suggested to Don Sabastiano that perhaps the dog had not swallowed the ring.

I accompanied Don Sabastiano back to Tenth Street. Peanuts ran on ahead, happy to be going home and oblivious to the worry that he was causing the old man.

On our return to his apartment, Don Sabastiano opened a can of dog food with the rusty kitchen knife he used for that purpose (his can opener had broken weeks before and he had never replaced it). Don Sabastiano's mood had suddenly changed. "By damn," he said angrily, "it's inside you, mutt, and I'm going to get it out! I'm not going to feed you till I do!"

With that, he began to collect chairs and cardboard boxes together and headed into the apartment bathroom.

"Help me," he said. "Bring his water and food dish over here." The old man secured the chairs and boxes across the doorway so that Peanuts couldn't get out. Then he placed the dog inside the bathroom with an ample supply of newspapers and the bowl of water.

"You're not going to eat until you crap that ring out!" Don Sabastiano boomed. He was angrier than I had ever seen him.

"I don't have to take this from you, Peanuts," he said. *"And the Lord said, Take now thy son, thine only son Isaac, whom thou lovest, and get thee into the land of Moriah.* Genesis, Twenty-two, Two."

He scowled at the dog. "Do you hear me, Peanuts? You know what that's about. Either you crap that ring out or we'll get it out the hard way!"

I told Don Sabastiano that I had to leave. I hated to see him angry. He starts threatening and you never know when he'll turn on you. As I left, I saw that he had pulled out a bottle of Thunderbird wine and was beginning to pour himself a drink.

I spent the rest of the afternoon writing in my office. It was the first time I really had a chance to write, and decided that I had put off starting my novel long enough. I plopped myself down in the burrow I had dug and placed a piece of eight by ten-inch white paper in the typewriter.

I had thought quite a bit about what kind of novel I should write and had settled on a love story. I knew that love stories were big in Hollywood and I figured that a love story would assure that some producer would want to make the novel into a movie right away.

"Got to think Master Plan, always think Master Plan," I said to myself.

The week before, I had taken Don Sabastiano into my confidence and had told him I was going to write a great love novel. He was immediately interested.

"What exactly do you know about love, *m'ijo?*" he asked. We were sitting on the steps of the apartment, taking in a really nice afternoon wind that blew in the smell of orange blossoms from the neighboring yard.

"Well," I said. "I know that men and women fall in love, and that they kiss a lot, and then they get married, and the guy sticks his thing into the woman, and then a baby comes out, and then they lived happily ever after."

"Well, there's more to it than that," he said. "Here, you should be taking notes. Wait up." He went into his apartment and returned with a small notebook and a pencil. He handed them to me.

"If you're going to be a writer, you have to get into the habit of taking notes."

He was absolutely right!

I had read where all great writers did research and took notes. I opened the notebook and wrote down "Notes On Love" at the top of the page. Then I turned to Don Sabastiano. "I'm ready," I said, getting comfortable on the porch.

Don Sabastiano talked all afternoon about love. He started with the different kinds of love: the love of God for human beings; the love of a mother for her child; the love of a leader for his people; the love of a brother for a brother; then he went on to boy/girl love. That's what I wanted to hear about. So he talked about that a lot. He talked and talked and talked, all afternoon long. And I took lots of notes.

Now, I pulled out my notebook and looked over what I had written that afternoon:

LOVE. A passionate feeling lasting a long time.
LOVE. The physical attraction of two people.
LOVE. The communion of two like souls.
LOVE. What keeps you going.

The last one is something that Don Sabastiano had said to me when I had asked him to define love. That's all he had said, no quote from the Bible or anything like that, just simply: "It's what keeps you going."

Now, the protagonist of my novel was a young woman not unlike Julia Miranda. I had to make it fit her so the studio executives would see how perfect she was for the part.

Anyway, in my novel the Julia character (whom I had named Yoli, just to spite Yoli Mendoza when the book came out) had just arrived in Hollywood and was befriended by an elderly gentlemen whose dear wife had died and had taken a fatherly interest in Julia—I mean Yoli!

I had gotten through the first two pages of the novel, getting my character to Hollywood, off the train, and settled in a modest apartment, when I developed writer's block. I knew I must have been doing something right because all the great writers I had read about developed writer's block every now and then.

I decided to quit for the day, went upstairs, and told my mom I had developed a bad case of writer's block and probably couldn't write for a day or two. My mother said that was too bad, but since I had time on my hands, I could run down to the Chino store and get groceries for tomorrow's lunch.

○ ○ ○

The next day I didn't see much of Don Sabastiano or Julia. I did keep my ears open for the sound of Julia's apartment door opening. I wanted to try the blue powder again, just in case it hadn't taken the first time. But every time I heard her door and ran outside, she was already down the sidewalk on her way out or already back inside her apartment.

That night our family went on an outing to visit the *compadres*, Braulio and Hortencia Moreno, and their three brats. Usually we go on Saturdays, but last Saturday, on account of all the commotion at Mrs. Romero's, we didn't go. So we were going to pay them a Wednesday-night visit.

The Morenos lived across town, and I hated going over there. There was absolutely nothing for me to do.

Hairy-chested Braulio and his fat wife Horetencia would sit in the kitchen with my mother and father and they would talk for hours while my sisters, María and Mónica, would play with the Moreno brats, Gloria, Sonia, and Eddie.

There was no one my age to play with, so I'd usually sit in the cab of our truck and take notes for my novel or think of Julia.

This trip was no different, though it was shorter because it was a weekday. We didn't get there until seven in the evening, and at ten my 'Apá woke me up in the cab where I had been sleeping and told me to get in the back because we were going home.

The next day I was determined that I'd make up for lost time and really get some writing done. I spent most of the day under the house, in my office, writing.

About four in the afternoon, my 'Apá came home from work, and that's when things really started to get hot. No sooner had he walked through the door than he and my mother were at it again. They started shouting at each other, real loud.

My sisters were playing outside, so I guess my folks thought they wouldn't hear them arguing. They didn't know I was under the house listening to every word they said.

"Come on, Refugia," my father roared, "it's not like I'd be doing anything illegal."

"*¡Cómo no!*" she shouted back. "What if he uses your truck and something happens?"

"But I won't be driving," my father replied. "I'm not even going to be there!"

"It's wrong, Horacio," my mother said. "You know it and I know it! I don't care if he is our *compadre*, it's unfair of him to ask you. If he gets caught, who're they going to come after?"

"But he won't get caught. He'll leave in the afternoon and have the truck back by noon the next day. And we'll make some money on it!"

My mind raced as I tried to figure out what the heck they were talking about. What scheme had *compadre*

Braulio come up with that that could get my 'Apá in such a jam for just loaning him the truck? This was all news to me.

Just then I heard Julia and Lizard Face enter her apartment. They were giggling and laughing and making quite a lot of noise. Pretty soon they were making so much noise they were drowning out my parents. I decided I'd go over and see what Julia and Spitface were up to.

I could hear them giggling upstairs. "No, Miguel!" I heard Julia raise her voice. "Do we have to go through that again?"

"*Ay*, come on, *chula*."

The weasel was at it again! He was trying to get her to drop her *chones* so he could stick it in her. But my Julia was sticking by her guns.

"Miguel, I'm not taking any chances!" she said emphatically. I felt good. That's telling him! I thought.

"Just this one time, *m'ija*? Just one time."

"One time? I don't know..."

Just then I heard the sound of a bottle breaking, but it wasn't coming from Julia's apartment. I looked down the length of the building and figured that the sound must have come from Don Sabastiano's. I decided I'd better investigate.

As I crawled over to his apartment, I could hear my father and mother still arguing at the top of their lungs.

"I don't care if they are illegals, they're still human beings. And it's not right what the *compadre* is doing!"

"But he *is* my *compadre*. I can't just tell him no!"

"You can if you want to keep the peace in this house!"

As I got to the area under Don Sabastiano's apartment, I noticed a shaft of light coming from overhead. The water dripping from the bathroom sink had rotted the wooden floor. I crawled over and saw that there were good-sized cracks in the flooring through which the bathroom light was shining.

I put my eye up close to one of the cracks and looked inside. Don Sabastiano was pacing in front of the bathroom, yelling at Peanuts.

"Miserable beast!" he shouted. "I saved you from the dog pound, fed you, and this is how you repay me? You'll pay for this, you little cur. You'll pay dearly for this!"

I adjusted myself under the cracks in the floorboard so I could see better. Boy, Don Sabastiano was really angry! He had that same cold look in his eyes that he had the time he tore down my mother's laundry.

He continued to pace back and forth, berating the dog. I could tell from the way he talked that he was drunk. He walked over to the bureau and picked up a photo of his wife.

He returned with the photo to the kitchen table where he picked up a nearly empty bottle of wine. He stared moodily at a photo of his departed wife and finished off the bottle. Now he was mumbling to himself.

"The only thing that you left for me, and that damn dog has taken it!" I could see that the wine was making Don Sabastiano really mean. He approached the make-shift corral.

"Damn you!" he said angrily. "I'm going to get that ring out of you if its the last thing I do!" Inside the corral, Peanuts was lying on his side. I knew Don Sabastiano had not fed him anything but water for two days. He looked up weakly at his master and managed a feeble wag of his tail.

The old man finished the bottle and threw it against the wall in disgust. It shattered with a loud crash and forced me to duck involuntarily.

"What was that?"

"It's just the old man next door, *chula*. Nothing to worry about. Come on, I'm taking precautions! You know you want to..."

"But..."

Don Sabastiano went into the kitchen and returned with another bottle of wine. He continued to pace back and forth in front of the bathroom. "You're doing this on purpose, you damn hound," he said. "Well, I've had enough. Look at you! I'm going to finish this once and for all!"

Don Sabastiano walked out of sight into the kitchen. Underneath the house I began to get worried. In the background I could hear my parents still arguing.

"Well, Horacio, you decide. But I'll tell you one thing: if the *migra* comes snooping around asking questions, I'm not going to tell any lies! I'm going to tell them that it was you and the *compadre* who did it!"

I watched in horror as Don Sabastiano returned and stood in front of the bathroom, brandishing a large kitchen knife. "*And Abraham stretched forth his hand,*" he said, "*and took the knife to slay his son.*"

I was terrified.

As I tried to get a better view, I noticed something glittering in the dirt next to me. The shafts of light coming through the cracks in the floor were reflecting on something that glistened on the ground. I stooped to pick it up and examined it in the light coming from above. I couldn't believe my eyes. It was Don Sabastiano's lost gold ring!

I realized then what had happened—the ring had fallen through the cracks in the floorboard. Peanuts hadn't swallowed it after all! Just then I noticed that Don Sabastiano was moving the chairs and cardboard boxes out his way as he approached the helpless canine. He still held the knife in his hand.

"Enough of this!" He yelled. "I'm through waiting for you to crap out that ring!"

I got so panicked that I sat up, knocking my head on the floorboards. Boy, did that hurt! I knew I had only a few moments to act if I was going to save Peanuts. I yelled at the top of my lungs: "Don't do it! Don't do it!"

In the neighboring apartment, I heard a loud crash. It sounded as if Miguelito and Julia had fallen off her couch and onto the floor.

"Miguelito, there's someone else in here."

"Damn, just when..."

I crawled toward the ventilation entrance as fast as I could, still calling from underneath the floorboard, "Don't do it! Don't do it!"

"Miguelito, someone's spying on us!"

Upstairs, my father stopped his tirade. "Don't do it? Where's that coming from? *Por Dios*, someone's been listening to us?"

"Well, I hope it was the *migra*," my mother said indignantly. "You can't do it now, someone knows!"

I reached the ventilation door and crawled out, still holding onto the gold ring and still calling out as loud as I could, "Don't do it! Don't do it!"

By the time I ran to the front of the apartment, the whole place was in an uproar. I headed toward Don Sabastiano's at a dead run, passing my mother and father as they came out of our doorway and nearly tripping over Julia as she came out of her apartment buttoning her blouse.

"Choo Choo, you little creep," Julia swore at me.

"What's going on?" my father shouted behind me.

I burst into Don Sabastiano's apartment and ran to the bathroom. As I careened to a stop at the doorway, I stopped dead in my tracks.

My mind was racing.

Suddenly I was trying to make sense of what I had expected to find and the surprising sight before me: Don Sabastiano stood in the bathroom quietly opening a can of dog food with the kitchen knife.

"I've had enough of this," he said to Peanuts. "I'm going to feed you, ring or no ring!" He finished the task and dumped the dog food into Peanuts' dish. "Got to get a new can opener," he said to himself as he wiped the knife clean on a paper towel. The dog immediately got up and began to eat.

"You're going to eat and that's that!" the old man said affectionately to the weiner dog. Then he noticed me standing there. "Hi, *m'ijo*, what're you doing here?"

I stared in disbelief as Peanuts ate his meal. "You weren't going to kill him after all?" I asked.

Don Sabastiano looked at me in surprise.

"Kill Peanuts? Why should I kill Peanuts?" Don Sabastiano asked, still holding the kitchen knife.

"But the ring..." My voice faltered.

"He can't have the ring in him. If he did, he would have crapped it out long ago. And no need to starve the dog."

That's when I remembered that I had the ring in my hand. "Look, Don Sabastiano," I said. "I found the ring!"

○ ○ ○

The next day my 'Apá made me move my office out from under the house and into a corner of the room I shared with my sisters. Boy, was he mad! That really cramped my writing style. Try writing something good with two bratty sisters looking over your shoulder! But that wasn't the worse of it.

My 'Apá made me apologize to Julia and Miguelito—spit in his face—and to promise never to listen to people's private conversations again. I didn't care so much about moving the office, but having to say I'm sorry to the Weasel was really humiliating. And in front of Julia!

My 'Apá never mentioned the argument about loaning *compadre* Braulio the truck, but he must have decided not to do it because after that we stopped going to visit the Morenos every Sunday the way we did before. I think they had a falling out.

A month later, Julia decided to leave the apartment and make her big move to Los Angeles. She and Weasel had gotten into a big fight, and he hadn't even volunteered to see her off. What a *sinvergüenza*!

But all this was great news for me! It was my big
chance to show my love for her and try out the love medicine once more. I didn't waste any time on it. As soon as
I overheard my 'Amá tell la señora Romero that Julia
was leaving and that she and Miquelito had broken up,
I raced to Julia's door.

She answered the door and stepped out on the
porch, right into the semicircle of magic powder. I could
see that she had been crying. I asked her if I could carry
her suitcase to the Greyhound depot. She looked surprised and then smiled. "Of course!" she said. "I'd like
that a lot." The medicine was working.

I was going to see her off myself!

○ ○ ○

On the morning that Julia was to leave, I went over
to Don Sabastiano's and confided to him about my love
for Julia. I told him I didn't know what to do. It was
going to be impossible for me to win her love now that
she was going to Hollywood to become a star.

"Well," he said to me. "It's going to be harder to win
her love from way out here in Arroyo Grande, that's for
sure," he agreed with me. "But it's not impossible. Nothing's impossible if you set your mind to it. You never
know what the future will bring."

"Well, should I tell her that I love her now?" I asked
him.

"What can it hurt?" he replied. Oh, this was going to
be the hardest thing I ever had to do.

That afternoon, I walked with Julia from the house
at 301 Tenth Street all the way to the Greyhound bus
depot on the corner of Main and Sixth Street. Eight
blocks in all, I counted them.

All during the walk I didn't say much. I was too nervous. My stomach was hurting really bad and my face
was sweating, even though it was an overcast afternoon
and cold.

Julia was wearing a coat and she was still shivering. She kept going on and on about how the next time she returned to Arroyo Grande, she would be a star.

"I'll be so famous," she said, "that they'll have a parade down Main Street just for me."

I shifted the suitcase from one hand to the other. Boy, it felt like it was full of bricks!

"And you know what, Choo Choo?" she continued.

"No, what?" I replied.

"I'm going to ride in that parade in a big gold Cadillac, and the only person I'm going to let ride with me is going to be you!"

Boy, that made me choke. Fortunately, we arrived at the Greyhound depot then, so I didn't have to say anything back to her. She went in and bought her ticket. I took her suitcase and gave it to the driver who stored it in a compartment under the bus. Julia came out and the bus driver nodded for her to get on board.

"Running late, Miss," the driver said to her as he climbed up the steps to take his seat.

Julia turned to say goodbye to me. My face was hot, my eyes were burning, and my stomach really hurt. But I knew that it was now or never.

I walked up to her and as coolly as I possibly could I said, "Julia, I love you and someday I will marry you."

She nodded her head and smiled at me. "I know you do," she said, "and maybe someday you *will* marry me. Why do you think I wanted you to carry my suitcase?"

Then she stooped down, put her arms around me, closed her eyes, and gave me a kiss. It wasn't the goodbye kiss on my cheek that I had expected, the kind I get from my Aunt Lucía or other adults. No, she gave me a long passionate kiss on my mouth.

I could feel her tongue moving smoothly across my teeth, and then touching here and there inside my mouth, and then her teeth biting my lips gently. It went on for the longest time, minutes and minutes! Then she

stopped, looked deep into my eyes, turned, and boarded
the bus.

As the bus drove off, I remembered to start breath-
ing again. All I could think of for the days and weeks
that followed was that the *medicina de amor* had
worked. Julia Miranda, the woman I loved, the woman I
would someday marry, had kissed me on the mouth like
an adult!

The Return
of Pancho Villa

The Return of Pancho Villa

The fly landed on the kitchen counter with the delicate grace of a ballerina. It pirouetted once, its iridescent wings shimmering as they reflected the afternoon sun coming through the kitchen window, then it began a slow, rocking dance as it inched along the porcelain edge of the sink. Now and then it would stop, wash its wings with its tiny feelers, then resume the staccato rhythm of its leisurely rumba.

I was creeping up on the fly, about to send it to that great ballroom in the sky with Mrs. Romero's plastic yellow flyswatter, when suddenly a shout jolted me out of my concentration.

"Yoli, don't you dare!"

It was Mrs. Romero herself, standing by the door that led from the living room into the kitchen, hands on her ample waist, and giving me a reprimanding glare that could melt lead.

"Huh?" I replied.

I was so unsettled by her shouting at me that I dropped the flyswatter and the fly escaped into the other room.

"You made me miss it," I said, picking up the flyswatter.

I hate it when I get thrown off that way. Mrs. Romero is probably the finest, most gentle and thoughtful lady in Arroyo Grande, and she had never once raised her voice at me. I guess that's why I was so startled. What had her so upset?

"*M'ija*, you shouldn't be killing flies," she said, softening the tone of her voice but keeping it firm enough for me to know she still meant business.

"What's wrong with killing flies?" I asked indignantly. "Mom does it all the time!"

"It's not good to needlessly kill any of God's creatures, not even a simple fly. God doesn't like it."

She walked into the kitchen and began to dry the dishes I had washed earlier. Ever since the day of the sinkhole, I had been coming by once a week to help Mrs. Romero clean her house, on account of her rheumatism (and because my mom would kill me if I didn't.). Mrs. Romero always insisted on helping me with the work. I think she enjoyed the company more than anything else.

"If God didn't want us to kill flies, why did he allow flyswatters to be invented?" I asked pointedly, wiping dead fly remains off the flyswatter with a paper towel.

She didn't say anything, just continued drying the dishes.

Must have got her good, I thought, because she was not even answering, probably trying to think up a comeback. To rub it in just a little bit, I kept cleaning the flyswatter that had bubbled out of the ground that Saturday when all hell broke loose on Fourth Street.

What a day that had been! I had hit a home run during morning practice with the Arroyo Grande Sluggers and then had shown Jeannie de la Cruz, the only other girl on the team, how to slide into home base. Reymundo, the team captain, had gotten mad at me.

"That's my job," he'd said, all indignant. "Around here I give the orders."

"So, show her how to slide home," I told him, getting a little hot myself. What does he know about how girls should slide into home base? I think he was just mad because he likes to feel that he's the boss.

Anyway, it turned out to be a great chance to break the ice with Jeannie, who'd been standoffish with me since she joined the team a month ago. After practice we all headed over to Mrs. Romero's to see the biggest hole that ever hit Arroyo Grande.

Mrs. Romero had told the whole gang—Reymundo Salazar, Bobby Hernández, Tudi Domínguez, Choo Choo Torres, Junior Valdez, Beto Armenta, Robert and Johnny Rodríguez, Smiley Rojas, Jeannie de la Cruz, and myself—that we could have anything we wanted from the large pile of junk that came out of the sinkhole.

By the end of the day, we all had something to take home. I wound up with a pair of mirrored sunglasses, a walking cane with a carved dragon handle (for my *abuelito* Tomás), and a Max Factor makeup kit, which I kept hidden from the other kids.

Mrs. Romero herself had picked up three items: the yellow flyswatter that I had been using, an orange food dish for her dog Junior, and a Pérez Prado album.

Anyway, Mrs. Romero didn't answer my question right away; she just kept drying dishes. Maybe I shouldn't have been so rude, I thought.

Now, don't get me wrong. There's nothing I like better than a good debate. That's my favorite fun, especially when I consider my opponent unarmed, like roly-poly, pea-brained ignoramus Bobby Hernández or halitosis-breath Big Bertha. Talk about an unfair fight—I leave them in the dust! *¡Qué mensos!*

But Mrs. Romero was another thing.

I respected her. She'd been married three times, had outlived her three husbands, and, heck, I figured that must count for something. I had to admit also that she usually had something worthwhile to say about one thing or another. Truth of the matter was I didn't really want to get into a verbal fight with her.

"God made flyswatters so that you could have the choice not to kill his creatures," Mrs. Romero said finally. "Free will, *m'ija*. That is what God has given you."

Oh great, I thought, free will! I wasn't quite sure I understood what it all meant, but I knew that I sure liked killing flies.

"But the most important reason for not killing flies," she continued, looking up from where she sat and fixing me with those clear grey eyes of hers, "is because when you kill flies, you are killing the soul of one of your ancestors."

"Ancestors? What're you talking about?" I asked, hanging the flyswatter on a nail in the back of the kitchen door. This was a new one on me.

"Don't you know that *moscas* are no more nor no less than the souls of dead ancestors who have passed on?" she asked. "They try to reach out to us from the great beyond."

"Go on!" I told her. "Where'd you hear that? Or did you just make it up?" It sounded to me like something she would make up just to get me to stop killing flies.

"I didn't *hear* it," she replied patiently, "and I didn't make it up. It's common knowledge—ask anyone. Now, haven't you ever been pestered by a *mosca*, buzzing around your ears at a picnic, at dinner, or when you want to be left alone?"

"Yeah, so what," I said, getting drawn into her story despite myself.

"Well, why do you suppose that fly is so determined to get to you? *M'ija*, that fly is the soul of some dead ancestor trying to speak to you. Most people are so busy, of course, or self-centered that they never listen."

"Well, what do the flies say?" I asked.

"They're trying to warn you about something, usually."

"Warn me?" I asked. "About what?"

"*M'ija*, our ancestors can see into the future. It comes with being dead. They know everything that has happened and everything that is going to happen. Souls can go forward and backward in time, you see. So, they can tell what is going to happen *si haces esto*, and they can tell what is going to happen, *si haces lo otro*. They try to tell you not to do this, or that you should do that."

"You don't expect me to believe all this *mosca* business," I said right back to her. "Really! I suppose they talk in *mosca* language, right? Buzz, buzz, buzz."

"Make all the fun you wish, *m'ija*," she said. She had finished the dishes. Now she hung the dish towel out to dry on a magnetic hook attached to the side of the refrigerator. "Someday you'll make a big mistake in life. You'll jump left when you should have jumped right, and all because you didn't listen to the *moscas*.

"For all you know," she continued as she ambled into the living room, "one of those flies may be the soul of your dear departed *tío*, Pancho Villa. *Que en paz descanse*."

Oh great, Pancho Villa!

According to tradition, our family was distantly related to the Mexican revolutionary, General Pancho Villa. He was supposed to have been a first cousin to my grandfather's first cousin or aunt or something like that—I never had gotten it straight. Ever since I could remember, everyone in our family always spoke of him as *Tío* Pancho Villa. They were real proud 'cause he was a famous general that defended the poor and had won many battles.

Anyway, I was determined not to let Mrs. Romero pull one over on me. "Oh," I said sarcastically, "so now I have the blood of my *tío* Pancho Villa on my hands?"

"No," she replied from the living room, "but you may have the *soul* of Pancho Villa on your hands."

I checked the clock on the kitchen stove and saw that it was almost four o'clock—time for Slugger baseball practice. I headed out the back door.

"Gotta go to baseball practice, Mrs. Romero," I shouted into the living room.

"What about the mambo lesson?" she called back. I had forgotten about that. I love dancing, and Mrs.

Romero, who could really clean up the dance floor in her day, had volunteered to show me how to mambo.

"I'll come by tomorrow," I shouted as I went out the back door. Then, just because I hate for anyone else to have the last word, I added, "And I don't need anyone telling me how to live *my* life! Not even Pancho Villa!"

○ ○ ○

"I don't hear a thing," Smiley Rojas said, holding his cupped hands tightly together close to his right ear.

It was later in the afternoon, and the Sluggers had gathered around the large plastic trash cans in my back yard. I had told them about what Mrs. Romero had said about flies being our dead ancestors.

Reymundo and Choo Choo were playing catch, Jeannie, Bobby and Smiley were taking turns with Smiley's new Hula-Hoop (the one he'd picked up at Mrs. Romero's sinkhole), and the rest of us—Junior, Beto, myself and the Rodríguez twins—were sprawled out on the grassy knoll behind the trash cans. I was only half paying attention to the fly experiment because all I could think of was the upcoming graduation dance. I had been agonizing about it for weeks and still couldn't think of a way out.

Smiley had spent the last ten minutes catching the fly which he now held in his hand and whose buzzing he was trying to interpret. We had decided to test out Mrs. Romero's idea that flies were, in fact, our dead ancestors sent down to earth to warn us of something.

Smiley listened again and then shook his head, "Nope, not a thing."

"So, just what's it supposed to be saying?" Reymundo Salazar asked sarcastically, tossing the baseball to Choo Choo who caught it with one of the leather gloves that Reymundo had picked out of Mrs. Romero's sinkhole.

"It can be saying anything," I replied, brushing hair away from my mirrored sunglasses. I loved wearing them because nobody could see my eyes and they made me look like a gangster. Any little edge on the guys is always appreciated.

Anyway, I was really torn about this graduation-dance business. I wanted to go because I love dancing. But what I didn't want to do was go through all the baloney of getting dressed up in a fancy dress. Most of all, I was determined that I wasn't going to act like a dithering idiot, like all the other girls at school.

Smiley strained to hear something intelligible from the angry buzzing of the fly in his cupped hands. "Do they communicate in Spanish or in English?" he asked.

"Maybe it's in Morse Code," Jeannie said. "You know, each buzz a dot or a dash." We had gotten to be better friends since my sliding-into-home base lessons, and I could see she was trying to back me up.

Junior Valdez pointed the weird space gun he had gotten from Mrs. Romero's at Jeannie, then at Smiley, then at the rest of us. Then he said, "I'm not really a Mexican. I'm really from outer space. I'm only temporarily occupying the body of Junior Valdez in Arroyo Grande until my spacecraft can be repaired. Then I'll return to the planet Zathar where I belong."

Junior was like that, always saying something totally off the wall and bizarre when you least expected it. I told you he's a real space nut!

"Here, let me listen," I said, ignoring Junior. I reached over with cupped hands and Smiley carefully passed the buzzing fly to me.

"Hey, Yoli," said Bobby, "in what country is the Amazon River located? Bet you don't know."

"Brazil," I snapped. "And get over it, Bobby."

I was in no mood for games. Ever since he'd picked up a world globe from the sinkhole that Saturday, Bobby had become a self-styled expert on world geography.

What he was doing, of course, was memorizing all the capitals, rivers, and countries on the globe.

Every now and then he'd ask me a question out of the clear blue to see if he could show me up in front of the others. Of course, being the dumb ignoramus that he is, it didn't occur to him that since the globe had been made in 1975, many of the countries and capitals were changed. I was just waiting for him to spring one on me that had changed, and then I'd have him!

I put the hands up to my ear and opened up a tiny space between my two thumbs and listened very hard. For the longest time all I could hear was the angry buzzing of the fly.

Reymundo and Choo Choo were looking at me like I was crazy. The rest of the gang looked like they expected me to say something to prove Mrs. Romero was not off her rocker. I knew Reymundo was just waiting for me to say that I couldn't hear anything so he could lord it over me. Being team captain, he thinks he can act like he's king of the mountain whenever he wants.

I was about to admit defeat when suddenly I heard it—a real tiny, tiny voice coming from deep inside my hand!

I looked up really startled. "I can hear a voice!" I said. Immediately Bobby, Jeannie, Smiley, and Junior crowded around me, trying to listen. I motioned them away.

"Shush!" I said.

I listened carefully and, sure enough, I could hear a voice, a real tiny voice. It was as if the voice were coming from the far side of a vast universe in the palm of my hand.

"Yoli," it said. "Yoli Mendoza. I need to talk to you! Listen to me!" It was speaking to me. The fly was actually saying something I could understand!

I angled my cupped hands closer to my ear to see if it would help me hear the voice any better. "Yes, I can

hear you, I can hear you!" I said. "Do you
am?" the voice asked.

"No," I replied. "Who are you and w
want?"

"I'm your_*tío*, the great General Pancho Villa. I have
come to advise you about something very important."

I couldn't believe this was happening.

Mrs. Romero had been right! I held the soul of my
Tío Pancho Villa in my hand and he was talking to me. I
turned to the gang that was crowding around me trying
to hear.

"I can hear my *Tío* Pancho Villa!" I said. "It's my *Tío*
Pancho Villa talking!"

"Go on, Yoli," said Reymundo guffawing. "You're just
saying that! You can't hear a darn thing!"

"Yes, I can...shush," I said, going back to my cupped
hands and trying to make out the buzzing. "You guys
are going to have to be quiet. He doesn't speak very
loud."

"Hey, how come Smiley couldn't hear anything and
now suddenly you can?" Reymundo asked.

"Yes, *Tío*?" I said, ignoring Reymundo. "What's that?
Oh I see. Wait a minute, *Tío*."

I turned to the gang. "My uncle, Pancho Villa, says
that I should tell that wise ass," I indicated Reymundo,
"that the reason why Smiley couldn't hear me and I can
is that he's *my* ancestor. If Smiley were to find a fly that
is the soul of one of *his* ancestors, then he'd be able to
hear him perfectly well."

"Very neat," Choo Choo said scornfully, "And what is
your Uncle Pancho Villa telling you now?"

I listened some more to the tiny voice in my hand.

"He's here to help me make decisions about my
future."

"What kind of decisions?" Reymundo asked.

"Yeah, like what?" Bobby echoed.

"Ask him a question," said Jeannie.

"Yeah, let him prove he's Pancho Villa."

"I will if you just give me a chance," I said. Then I spoke back into my cupped hands. "*Tío*, what is it that you want to advise me about?"

I put my ear close to my cupped hands and listened. Far off, I could hear the tiny voice speaking. "The dance," the voice said. "It's about the graduation dance. You *must* go!"

"The graduation dance?" I asked out loud.

A cold shiver rippled up my back. Nobody, but nobody, knew how upset I was about the graduation dance. For weeks I had kept it all to myself. But now, somehow this fly, or my Uncle Pancho Villa, or whoever or whatever it was, suddenly knew my innermost secret.

I was so startled that I let my hands open and the fly flew out.

"Hey, you let it go!" Bobby yelled, trying to grab the fly as it buzzed by him.

I watched as the fly returned to the swarm gathered around the trash cans. I was in shock. I sat down on the grass and tried to make sense of this.

How could anyone know about the most horrible problem I'd faced in months?

The sixth-grade graduation dance, which Mrs. Grath had announced several weeks ago, was the traditional event that for years had marked the transition of sixth graders from Arroyo Grande Elementary School to seventh grade at Jefferson Junior High.

Since the announcement, all of the girls in my class had gone bananas. All they talked about was what dress they would wear, how they would make up their hair, what kind of makeup they would use, and what boy they'd like to dance with.

The girls in my class are real *pendejas*: too chicken to play a decent game of baseball or execute a simple ollie-to-sidewalk shred on a skater. Little princesses with their stupid flirty smiles and giggly looks at the boys! And all of them swooning every time Johnny Montgomery, the one gringo kid in class, walked by. I really don't know what they see in him. Yeech, it makes me wanna puke!

Since the announcement of the graduation dance, my life had been hell. But it wasn't the other girls that were making my life miserable. It was my own friends, the guys on the baseball team. They had all agreed to go and wanted to know if I was going.

The thought of having to get dressed up in a fancy dress, with heels and a perm the way all the other girls were planning was enough to make me want to crawl under the covers of my bed and never come out. And yet I liked to dance!

But I couldn't just tell them that I wasn't going.

I knew all the Sluggers would be there, even Jeannie de la Cruz. So, I was in a real fix. The day of the dance was only a week and a half away, and I'd have to decide sooner or later to go or come up with some good excuse not to go, but then miss out on all my friends.

"The graduation dance?" Jeannie asked.

"What about the dance?" Choo Choo joined in.

I was still pretty shaken from what the fly had told me, so I said the first thing that came into my mind. "He said we shouldn't go to the graduation dance this year."

"What?" the Rodríguez twins chorused.

"Who shouldn't go?" asked Beto.

"None of us," I replied.

Reymundo stopped his game of catch. "Is there something that's going to happen at the dance?" He walked over to where I sat on the grass. "Huh, is there?"

"Yeah, why don't he want us to go to the dance?" piped up Bobby.

"I don't know. That was all he said," I replied. "You and your friends should not go to the dance next Friday. And that was it."

"How convenient," Choo Choo said. "Now that she let the fly go, she can make up everything it told her and we won't have any way of finding out if its true or not!"

"What else did he tell you, Yoli?" Bobby asked.

"Nothing," I said. "He flew away before he could tell me anything else."

"Aren't you gonna catch him again and find out?" Jeannie de la Cruz asked.

"I don't know which one he is," I said looking about the dozens of flies milling about the trash cans. "Anyway, that was probably all he had to say to me. That we shouldn't go to the dance."

"That's a bunch of baloney and you know it, Yoli. You're just making it up!" said Reymundo. "Well, I'm sure going to the dance, fly or no fly."

"Suit yourself," I said defensively. "I only report what I heard. As for me, I think if a fly comes all the way from wherever souls live to tell us not to go to the dance, then I think we should really listen up."

I looked at everyone and wondered why I had lied about what my *tío*, the fly, had said. But the lie was out. If I told them the truth, they'd really think I had made the whole thing up. Why did I lie? Because I didn't want to go to the stupid dance, that's why!

And what kind of *tío* was he anyway, telling me that I should go? Who's side was he on?

"But what if Yoli's right," said Jeannie, making it sound real sinister. "What if something terrible will happen to us if we do go to the dance? Like what if there's a fire or the roof of the building caves in or something like that? And we were warned?"

Well, that shut everyone up for a moment. We all sat quietly thinking about the fly and the dance and the terrible things that might occur.

"I'm not really of this space-time continuum," Junior Valdez said, breaking the silence. "The planet Zathar is located in a parallel universe, and that's why I'm stuck in the body of Junior Valdez. As soon as my spacecraft is fixed, I can accelerate to beyond warp speed, break the time/space barrier, and return home to my own universe."

We ignored him as usual.

"Yoli, you're just chicken," Beto started in again. "You just don't want to go to the dance and are trying to spoil it for everyone else."

I could've killed him!

I decided I'd better change the subject before things got more personal. "Anyway, what'd you say we go for cokes?" I said.

"Yeah," said Choo Choo, "let's go over to Junior's and see if his old man will spring for some freebies."

Junior's father, Mr. Valdez, ran the Mariposa Grocery store on Fifth Street, right across from Don Carlos Vásquez's empty lot where we play baseball. Now and then, when he was in a good mood, he'd treat us to cokes or ice-cream bars.

"Yeah, let's go," said Bobby, always at the front of any food line. "Hey, Yoli," he added, "what's the capital of Nigeria?"

"Lagos," I said authoritatively.

"You're right," said Bobby, as if only he knew the answer to the question. Just wait, he'd screw up sooner or later.

We picked up our skateboards and started out into the warm summer evening. As we skated to Mr. Valdez's store, I kept thinking to myself, he knows! My uncle, the fly, knows!

○ ○ ○

That evening Pancho Villa returned.

I was washing the dinner dishes when a fly started buzzing loudly about my head. I started to dry off my hands to see if I could catch it, but then I heard a voice as deep as the Grand Canyon say to me, "No need to catch me, I can make myself heard well enough."

"Is it really you?" I asked, still trying to believe all of this was really happening to me.

"Don't you believe your eyes and ears?" he said. "Don't you remember what your *abuelito* Tomás told you about me? The Battle of Torreón and of Zacatecas? I was there! That's me."

"Wow," I said, "it's just so unbelievable. I mean, first Mrs. Romero tells me about you flies and then here you are!"

"Not anymore unbelievable than a lot of things people believe these days. Anyway, I didn't come by for small talk. It's the dance I want to talk to you about."

"What about it, and how did you know…?"

"I know everything. So, what I came to tell you is that you must go to the dance, even though you're afraid."

"I'm not afraid!"

"Don't lie to me. I happen to know exactly what you're thinking at all times, even when I'm not around." The voice was coming in loud and clear as the fly zoomed around my head.

"*M'ija*," Pancho Villa continued, "you're afraid. You're afraid that when you show up at the dance, the boys in the Sluggers won't want to dance with you."

"That's not true,… " I started to say.

"Don't interrupt your elders," he continued. "You're also afraid that you'll look silly in makeup and that Big Bertha and Nellie Chávez will make fun of you when they see you dressed up."

"I don't care what Big Bertha and Nellie think," I told him.

And that *was* the truth.

I hadn't hung out with Big Bertha or Nellie or any of the other girls I used to be friends with in my sixth-grade class since the trainer-bra incident a couple of months ago. Heck, I didn't care what they thought of me.

"You're afraid that if you try to dance," he continued, "you'll make a fool of yourself. You're afraid that Choo

Choo Torres, on whom you have a secret crush, will ignore you throughout the dance.

"And most of all," he went on, "you're afraid that once the boys on the Sluggers see you dressed up in a dress, with a perm and the whole works, they won't want you to play second base for the team anymore."

That's when I stopped washing the dishes and started to cry. He was exactly right.

The whole thing about not being asked to dance, about sitting on the sidelines, about being laughed at by the other girls. All that was true.

But even worse than that, he was exactly right about my worst fear. What if the dance *changed* things? What if the boys decided they didn't want me on the team? I knew I was the best second baser they'd ever had, but what if?

"Well, what should I do?" I asked, wiping my face with soapy hands.

"If you follow my instructions, you'll do fine. First, you must decide in your mind that you *are* going. It's all in your attitude; that's how I won that little skirmish outside of Torreón in 1913. Then, you must prepare. Tonight, when everyone's watching TV, tell your mom you're going to take a bath. Go find that box you got out of Mrs. Romero's front yard and carry it into the bathroom. Lock the door and experiment."

"You know about the box?"

"Haven't you been paying attention? I said I know everything. Now, do as I say. Get the box." With that the fly flew out of the kitchen.

The box was the Max Factor kit that I had picked up at Mrs. Romero's. It contained a variety of colored blushes, eye liners, and mascara. Perhaps it was the dance that was in the back of my mind on that Saturday when Mrs. Romero's sinkhole exploded. Why else would I have picked up that Max Factor makeup kit in the first place?

And so, after I finished the dishes, I went into the bathroom for two hours and experimented with different lip stick colors, powdered blushes, and eye-liners.

I realized that my uncle, the fly, was right. If I had to go to the dance, then I'd better learn how to do this makeup stuff right.

I didn't dare tell Mom what I was doing. She'd been trying to get me to wear makeup for months.

"Ay, m'ija," she'd say, "when are you going to grow up like the other girls and become a young lady?" If Mom knew what I was doing, she'd have a laugh I'd never live down.

Besides, I thought, what can there be to makeup? If I can hit home runs and outrun Bobby Hernández to first base, I can master a simple makeup kit.

So I sat myself down in front of the bathroom mirror and started in. It was the first time I had ever consciously sat before a mirror and tried to make myself look attractive, and, honest to God, I wasn't very happy about it. Why do we women have to spend so much time on makeup? Boys don't have to do it! It's unfair!

But I was determined and I stuck with it. Before long I was able to put on lipstick without smearing myself and put pink blush in exactly the right spot to bring out the sharp rise in my cheekbones like the models had in the copy of *Glamour* magazine I'd seen at the market.

Then I practiced applying mascara to my eyelashes without getting bits caught in my eye. When I was finished, I was really surprised. To tell you the truth, I looked pretty good. I mean for someone with makeup. After that, I put away the makeup kit and washed my face thoroughly.

Now I knew I could look as much like a monkey as any of the other girls—big deal! After that, I took a quick shower and went to bed.

○ ○ ○

Early the next morning I was awakened by a buzzing around my head. It was Pancho Villa again, and he was back with more instructions. "You need to polish up your dancing," he said. "So I want you to go back to Mrs. Romero and take those mambo lessons she offered to give you."

"Mambo?" I said incredulously. "That's the last thing kids are going to be dancing! All the girls are practicing break-dance numbers, and moon walking, and hip-hop moves. Mambo is so old-fashioned it's not even on the map!" Bad enough I was agreeing to go to the dance, I didn't have to make a fool of myself.

"That's exactly why you're going to learn to mambo, and to cha-cha and to rumba. You wait and see, you're going to knock their socks off! *M'ija*, trust me on this."

So that afternoon Jeannie de la Cruz and I walked home from school together and I confessed to her that I had decided to attend the graduation dance. "That's great!" Jeannie replied with that big toothy smile of hers. "We can go to the dance together!"

"Jeannie," I said, "Mrs. Romero has offered to teach me some dance steps, wanna come along?"

"Mrs. Romero?" Jeannie asked.

"Yeah," I replied. "Believe it or not, she's really good."

"All right, sure!" Jeannie said enthusiastically.

I was so happy that I had found a true friend in Jeannie that I gave her a big hug right there and then.

When we got to Mrs. Romero, the old lady was really happy to see us and eager to teach us some of the dance steps from her youth. "*¡Cómo no, cómo no!*" she said. "I'll teach you everything I know!"

Jeanie and I spent the entire afternoon at Mrs. Romero's, and she showed us all kinds of dance steps. I didn't realize it, but the old lady was quite an expert. She must have been something to see in her day!

She started in with the cha-cha, and had Jeannie and I repeating out loud one-two and cha-cha-cha, one-two and cha-cha-cha. Then we moved on to other dances. It turned out that Mrs. Romero had quite a collection of records she had acquired over the years.

Many of them were by musicians I hadn't even heard of, like Machito, Luis Alcaraz, Benny Moré, and Pérez Prado. She also had more familiar musicians that occasionally were played on Chile Colorado, the local AM station—La Banda Móvil, Los Tigres del Norte, Los Bukis, and others.

We had so much fun that afternoon we decided that we'd come over to Mrs. Romero every afternoon until the day of the graduation dance.

○ ○ ○

The afternoon that Jeannie and I began our dance lessons with Mrs. Romero was the beginning of my long friendship with Jeannie. Before that we'd played together, but usually it was at Slugger practice or at some school event.

But on that day, and the days that followed as we continued to prepare for the graduation dance, something happened. We became good friends—I mean really *special* friends. The rest of the week was spent going over all that we might run into at the dance. We were both determined that we would outshine and outdo not only every Slugger present, but Big Bertha and Nellie Chávez and the rest of the hyenas in our sixth-grade class.

The dress and shoes were the tricky part. I finally broke down and told my mom that I had to go to the school dance and asked if she would help me find something that didn't look like it was the latest World War II fashion.

And you know what? She didn't laugh or bag on me about it. She just said, real matter of fact, "*M'ija*, don't you worry. We're going to make you the nicest dress that ever was." Just like that, as if I went to dances all the time.

So, we spent all day Saturday and Sunday at the house working on the dress. My mom measured me and cut patterns and sewed. I tried to help as much as I could, now that I was getting into it. But I'm not much good at sewing, so mostly I watched.

The most embarrassing part of it was when my mom started measuring my chest for the dress. She had the measuring tape around me and felt the tight elastic bra I was wearing.

"*M'ija*, she asked, "what are you wearing?"

I was mortified. Since my *chichis* had started to grow, I had taken to wearing an athletic bra with elastic so tight that it hugged my breasts to my chest. Try fielding a ground ball or beating Reymundo Salazar to the top of the rope climb with your *chichis* getting in the way! That's why I had gotten the running bra with the strongest elastic I could find. It kept them flat and out of the way. I wore it with a loose fitting sweatshirt every time the Sluggers practiced, and nobody even noticed that my *chichis* had grown.

"Don't ask, Mom," I said, cutting her off. "I'll get a regular bra this afternoon." And I did. I raided my clay piggy bank with the sombrero on top, marched myself down to Penney's, and got one that let my *chichis* breath a little. Boy, they felt huge in that thing!

I got together with Jeannie on Monday night and we practiced walking in our high heels. I had worn heels just once before, when I was ten and my mom had insisted on an Easter-Sunday church reception. Things had gone well until I fell on my face coming down the Church steps and skinned my knees. I had given up on them after that, and my mom had felt so bad about my skinned knees that she never bothered me about it again.

"If you expect to be able to walk in those by Friday, you're going to really need more practice," Jeannie said as she watched me wobble across her living-room rug.

She was right. I would take a step and then feel like I was on top of the Empire State Building about to fall. Can you get seasick from walking in high heels? Well, I almost did!

We got together Tuesday and Wednesday night as well, just to make sure I wouldn't fall walking into the school gym, where the dance was to be held.

All during this time, I hadn't heard a thing from Uncle Pancho Villa. I figured that he had finished his mission and had gone back to wherever the souls of our ancestors come from. But on the morning of the graduation dance, he returned.

It was mid-morning and I was busy finishing my makeup in the bathroom when I heard the fly buzzing around the room.

"There's just one more thing," the fly said.

"You're back!" I said surprised.

"Only for a moment. You're not the only descendent I have to watch over in this world. And, if you can believe this, the rest are worse off than you! Anyway, I have one more thing to say to you."

"Yeah," I said skeptically. By now the idea of this fly telling me how to live my life had kind of sunk in and all I was hoping was that, when all was said and done, he knew what he was doing.

"Hold your head high and don't take any *mierda* from anyone."

"What do you mean?" I said.

"What I mean is that there's a lot of idiots in this world and some of them will be at this dance," he replied. "There's always someone who will try to intimidate you or boss you around or make you feel inferior, just so they can feel good about themselves. You can't let that happen. Just stare them back square in the eye and don't back down."

"Is someone going to do something to me at the dance?" I asked, getting worried. "This kind of pep talk isn't exactly what I needed."

"Can't tell you," he replied. "I can only warn you."

"Great," I said, "you're a big help."

"Be yourself and don't take any *mierda* from anyone!"

With that, the fly buzzed out the bathroom and that was the last I ever saw of it!

○ ○ ○

The afternoon of the dance, Jeannie came by early to pick me up so we could walk to school together. I was just finishing up in the bathroom when Mom called out to me that Jeannie had arrived. Before going out, I took one last look at myself in the cracked bathroom mirror.

As I surveyed myself, I realized how different I looked.

My permed hair cascaded down in curls on both sides of my head and partially covered my shoulders that were exposed in the strapless evening gown Mom had made of blue silk and white chiffon fringe. The front of the dress fit snugly over my bra so that you could see just a bit of the top of my *chichis* under the fringe that laced the dress.

"You need to show a little cleavage, *m'ija*," my mom had said when I had first tried on the dress a few days before. "It's considered fashionable and not at all cheap."

Boy, she knew where I was coming from.

The high heels I was wearing made me look several inches taller, and the belt around my waist pulled in my stomach and made my breasts look even larger than they were. The combination of the dress, my new bra, the heels, black nylons, makeup, and the perm made me look old, I mean real old, like seventeen or eighteen or something.

I thought it was just my imagination, but when I walked into the kitchen where my mom was serving Jeannie some *buñuelos* with milk, I realized that it really was true.

"Yoli," Jeannie gasped when she saw me, "you look magnificent! I hardly recognize you!"

"*Ay m'ija, qué bonita te ves*," my mother echoed.

Jeannie picked up a pair of scissors from the sewing table still set up in the kitchen and came over to me. "You look like a high schooler already!"

She pulled some strands of hair and arranged them in wisps across my forehead, cutting here and there so they looked real casual. Then she showed it to me in the mirror. Boy, that made even more of a difference! Jeannie's good at that kind of stuff.

"You look like someone else," she kept saying. "You look like someone else!"

"Well, let's go," I said, anxious to get the whole thing over with. I had been nervous about this for so long that by now all I wanted was to get the dance over with so I could go back to being my old self.

Before we left the house, Mom made Jeannie and me stand side by side so she could take a picture with the family instamatic camera.

"*M'ija*," she said, "you'll cherish these photos when you grow older."

"Yeah, sure, Mom," I told her, "but can we go now?"

The graduation dance was set for five o'clock so that it could get dark during the course of the two-hours of the dance. That way, when it was over, we'd come out into the night, just like adult dances.

Jeannie and I took our time walking to the school, and still arrived early. Not wanting to appear too eager, we decide to hide out in the girl's restroom of the gym.

I felt as nervous as a cat in a roomful of rocking chairs and kept looking at myself in the mirror. I kept asking Jeannie if I looked okay.

"Just great," she kept saying. "They're not going to believe it's you, that's what."

We waited until 5:20. By then the bathroom was getting crowded with other girls, so we decided we might as well make our grand entrance. Just as we were leaving the bathroom, who should walk in but Big Bertha and Nellie Chávez.

And you know what? They didn't say a word, just walked right on past me as if I wasn't there. When we got outside, Jeannie tugged on my sleeves.

"Did you see that? I told you! They didn't even recognize you! They didn't even know it was you, Yoli!"

She was right! As I walked down the hallway toward the entrance of the gym, I saw Mrs. Grath coming our way. I smiled as she passed and said, "Hello, Mrs. Grath."

She stopped and turned and looked back at me with a puzzled look. Then I saw it, the look of recognition as she realized who it was. "Why it's Yoli!" she said, smiling back at me. "Yoli, you look...beautiful!"

Jeannie gave me an I-told-you-so look and we walked on to the gym.

We stopped at the doorway before going in. My *chichis* felt like they were going to jump out of my dress, but I took a deep breath and turned to Jeannie.

"Let's do it," I said.

Inside the gym it was dark. We stood by the door for a moment to let our eyes get accustomed to the lights which had been put on low dimmer. Overhead, a crystal ball hung from the center of the ceiling. As it twirled about, it cast reflections of the tiny dimmer lights all around the room.

As my eyes became accustomed, I saw that Bobby Hernández, Reymundo Salazar, and Choo Choo Torres were sipping punch from a glass bowl nearby. They were wearing white shirts and sweaters and their regular school pants. See how easy boys have it!

Jeannie and I walked over and joined them. "Hi, guys," I said, real casual-like.

You should have seen the look on their faces!

"Yoooli," Choo Choo said, almost gagging as he gulped his drink.

"Hi, Yoli," Reymundo said, trying to be cool. "Thought you weren't coming to the dance. Some disaster might happen, remember?"

"The evening ain't over yet," I replied.

Bobby didn't say anything. He just kept looking at my chest like he expected it to explode or something. Pretty soon all three of them were looking at my chest. They weren't saying anything, just standing there staring at my chest.

God, I thought, they must look enormous. But I didn't let on that it bothered me.

"You guys going to dance?" I asked, trying to break the spell.

"Sure, Yoli, I'll dance with you," Reymundo said.

"I'm not asking you to dance," I said defensively. "Just a general question, you know, like how's the weather. Anyway, boys are supposed to ask the girls."

"You look real nice in that dress," Bobby repeated, his eyes still glued to my *chichis*.

"We're going to walk around a bit," I said. "See you."

Bobby recovered from his surprise then because he started in with one of his stupid questions before we could walk away. "Hey, Yoli," he said, "what's the capital of the Belgian Congo?"

"There is no such country as the Belgian Congo," I said, coming right back him. "It's now called Zaire. Check it out in the library." And then I walked away, Jeannie following closely behind.

Bobby just stood there without a thing to say. Got him good! Well, showing Bobby up seemed to turn things around for me. Suddenly I wasn't afraid or nervous, just eager to enjoy the party. And the rest of the dance was just about the best time I ever had in the world!

The first dance tune up was Michael Jackson's *Billie Jean*. Everyone was standing around along the side of the walls, but no one was ready to go out and be the first one on the dance floor.

So Jeannie and I got out there and did a moonwalk routine we had practiced the week before. You should have seen the look on Big Bertha's face!

The next number was a rap song. By now a lot of kids were dancing, most of them just standing in one place, throwing their hands up in the air, and rocking to the music. Jeannie and I wanted to show off, so we did a mambo and then a cha-cha routine to the rap song.

The cha-cha routine caught on immediately. Pretty soon everyone was imitating us, doing one-two- and cha-cha-cha to the rap lyrics. By the end of the song we were leading the whole dance floor in a new cha-cha version of rap—we had invented a new dance!

I looked over to where the Sluggers were standing. Naturally, they weren't dancing; they were mesmerized. All they could do was stare at Jeannie and me in disbelief.

The next tune was a slow-dance number. Jeannie and I decided to find a couple of chairs and sit it out. We wanted to see if anyone would ask us to dance.

Well, imagine my surprise when up steps Reymundo Salazar, Beto Méndez, *and* Johnny Montgomery, the *gringuito* all the hyenas are crazy about, all getting to my chair at the same time and then fumbling about, tripping over themselves to ask me for the dance. I could have died!

I took Johnny up on the dance, of course, just to see the expression on Nellie's face—she's the one that had printed his name on her hand with an ink pen.

It was a slow dance, but Johnny didn't try anything with me. I mean, no grind or anything like that. (I don't think the gringos know that kind of dancing). Anyway, he was just real polite and friendly. We even talked a bit about how much fun it was going to be now that school was out and we could stay outside till late.

The rest of the dance was like that—with Reymundo and Choo Choo and Beto and the Rodríguez twins all hanging around me and Jeannie. We were like two princesses holding court. Now and then one of the guys would ask me or Jeannie to dance and we would. All except Choo Choo, who just sat in the chair next to me and didn't say too much but kept staring at me.

I danced at least once with everyone who asked me, just so no one would feel that I was shining them on or would have their feelings hurt.

After a while, the other boys except Reymundo stopped asking me to dance. So I danced with him a couple of times, then it hit me. The reason the other Sluggers weren't asking me to dance was because Reymundo had told them not to. He wanted me all to himself! Well, when I got wise to that, I started turning him down. "I'm getting tired," I told him. "Why don't you ask Jeannie?" What nerve!

And all this time Choo Choo, who I do think is real cute, just kept staring at me but wouldn't say a word, much less ask me to dance. I guess he must be really stuck on Julia Miranda, the neighbor he's always talking about.

The only time Choo Choo got up was when Nellie Chávez came walking by where we were seated and pretended to accidentally trip so she could spill punch on my dress. It was Choo Choo who jumped in front of me and got himself wet instead. How gallant, huh? Nellie just walked away, all bothered and mad.

Before long, Mr. Robbins, the school principal, was announcing the last dance and saying that there would be more punch and cookies served outside the gym as people left. Then he put on the last song and announced that, as was traditional, the last dance would be ladies' choice.

Well, of course, I asked Choo Choo to dance. And you should have seen the look on Reymundo's face. He was actually jealous!

Choo Choo sure seemed pleased that I had asked him, and we even talked a bit. Well, I did most of the talking. He just said, "Uh huh," and "Yeah, sure," about a hundred times. And of course, he was the worst dancer of all the guys I danced with that day. He kept stepping on my feet! Still, it felt good being close to him.

The number ended and Choo Choo thanked me and then hurried back to the Sluggers. Jeannie and I walked outside together, since now that the dance was over the boys were all acting like boys again, talking about the summer schedule of baseball practice.

I figured the best was over and that we should get home while we were ahead, but Jeannie kept saying, "Oh, come on, Yoli, let's take some of these cookies with us for later on."

How Jeannie can know so much about makeup and dresses and dancing and still be ready to pig out at the drop of a hat I'll never know.

I agreed, and we stopped by the cookie stand and ate some cookies, then put some more in our purses for later.

We were about a half-a-block away from the school, still laughing at how Big Bertha and Nellie had looked, and how the guys couldn't take their eyes off our *chichis*, when we heard the sound of someone running behind us. We turned and there was Reymundo running straight at us, calling out my name as he ran.

"Yoli," he said, "wait up!"

I figured something was wrong or that maybe I had forgotten something. But when he caught up with us, he just stopped running and stood there not saying anything, looking at me and then at Jeannie.

"I'll walk slowly and you can catch up with me," Jeannie said, walking away to leave me alone with Reymundo. Some friend. I wanted to kill her!

"Uh, Yoli..." Reymundo started to say. Boy, was he nervous. He was standing a foot away from me and I could hear his heart pounding.

"Uh, I just wanted to say..." he stammered, "uh, what I mean is." Then before I knew what was happening, he leaned over and kissed me.

I was so surprised that it was a full minute before I did anything. I mean his lips were on my lips, right on my mouth! His eyes were closed and he was holding my arms to my side. I had my eyes opened and was looking at him, wondering what was going on.

And then he stopped and pulled away and a slow smile crawled across his face. "I had to do that," he said.

Well, isn't that a heck of a way to end a perfectly nice evening!

Remembering my Uncle Pancho Villa's words, there was only one thing I could do and I did it. I swung my hand back as far as I could and slapped Reymundo across the face so hard that my hand hurt for a week! Who did he think I was anyway!

Attack of the Lowrider Zombies

Attack of the Lowrider Zombies

The black '49 Chevy Fleetline moved in slow motion through rush hour traffic with the ponderous grace of an ebony tortoise waddling through quicksand. The afternoon sun penetrated the thick film of smog that hung over traffic, reflecting off the car's polished veneer and making the vintage roadster shine with black iridescence. Now and then, a piece of the chrome bumper or polished door handle caught the sun at just the right angle to erupt in an explosion of dazzling sunlight like a sparkler on the Fourth of July.

It was the same Chevy Fleetline that I had pulled out of Mrs. Romero's sinkhole several months before. I had since rebuilt the engine, laid in new upholstery, and had decided that the car's maiden voyage would be from Arroyo Grande, Texas, to Los Angeles, California. Now, after two days of driving, I sat in rush-hour traffic, proud to be at the wheel.

I wore my usual black-on-black shirt and pant combination and the brown fedora that I had also picked up at Mrs. Romero's. We made quite a sight, me and the '49 Fleetline—I relished every stare I got from passing motorists.

I had arrived in Los Angeles only an hour earlier, at midafternoon, and realized I had some time to kill. The pretext for the trip had been to visit my cousin Raúl, whom I hadn't seen in ten years. But I knew that he didn't get off work until six. So, I decided some sightseeing was in order and made my way to the Hollywood Chinese Theater.

I remembered it as "Grauman's" Chinese Theater, but they had changed the name to "Mann's" Chinese Theater. It was the same one though, with tourists from Des Moines, Tokyo, and Mexico City trying to match their footprints and handprints with those of famous stars. The movie advertised on the marquee was "Invasion of the Body Snatchers, Part VI."

I walked around the theater for a while, bought some postcards for the folks back home, grabbed a hot dog and a coke, then decided it was time to head out to East Los Angeles and the long-awaited family reunion. Because of rush-hour traffic I figured I'd try surface streets and headed out on Santa Monica Boulevard.

I was waiting for the light to change at a stop light when I noticed a hitchhiker. He was standing by a bus stop, his right thumb in the familiar gesture and holding an open umbrella with his left hand. It had been cloudy all day, but it hadn't started to rain yet. But this guy had his umbrella open! What really drew my attention was his get-up. He wore a *charro* outfit with an enormous broad-brimmed Mexican sombrero, the kind you get at border tourist stores. Well, I thought, that's one way to catch the eye of passing motorists.

I decided to reward the *charro* outfit and pulled over to pick up the hitchhiker. I brought the Chevy to a stop a few feet ahead of him and swung open the passenger door. He folded his umbrella, got into the passenger seat, closed the door, nodded a smile to me, then reached over and turned off the radio. "No music, pleez," he said. Then he looked out the window as if to say, "Let's get this turkey on the road."

Just like that! Not even a "thank you for stopping," "where are you going" or "nice car you have." He just gets in, turns off the radio, and expects me to act like a chauffeur. *¡Qué huevos!*

I decided not to say anything and pulled the car back into traffic instead. As we drove along, I noticed that this guy had gone all the way on the *charro* outfit.

He looked like a real Mexican Revolutionary, you know, the kind you see in those old Pancho Villa movies. The pant legs of his leather *charro* pants were lined with the big silver buckles. Across his chest he wore two criss-crossed *bandoleras* full of bullets. They looked real. He even had a mustache that stuck out an inch and a half on the sides of his mouth. The strangest thing was his face. It was green.

I figured he must have some kind of weird makeup on—hey, in Hollywood anything is possible. Yeah, this guy was quite a sight. A real frito bandito, I thought to myself.

The other thing I noticed was his smell. Boy, this guy hadn't bathed in months, what a stench! *¡Puchi!*

"My name's Rudy," I offered, trying to ignore his body odor. "But my friends call me Bugs."

The hitchhiker acted like he hadn't heard me, so I said it louder. "My name is Rudy. What's your name?"

This time he responded. "My name, she ees Pancho." He spoke with the funniest sing-song accent I'd ever heard. It reminded me of the way they talked in the old Cisco Kid movies.

I decided to ignore his bad manners. "I'm heading out to East Los Angeles," I explained to him. "Where are you heading?"

"Oh, say-nyor, you pleez to making right turn here," he said with that same phony Mexican accent. At first I thought the accent was a put-on, but one look at his deadpan face told me that he was a real serious customer. I decided not to laugh and turned as requested. We were on Van Ness now, heading south.

"Sure, where exactly are you going?" I asked.

"Paramount, I teenk so," he said.

"Paramount?" I said. "I'm not sure where that is." I'd heard of the city of Paramount, but couldn't remember if it was south or east of downtown Los Angeles.

"Paramount *estudios*, pleez," he said.

"Oh, *studios*. You want to go to Paramount studios!"

Paramount Studios. Suddenly it all made sense to me, or so I thought at the time. His costume, his accent, the makeup, the gun—he must be an extra in some movie!

"Oh," I said. "You must be an actor! Why didn't you say so? I'm really interested in actors. A girl from my home town is out here someplace. Name is Julia Miranda. She's an actress, too. I mean, I think she must be by now. We haven't heard much from her since she came out here, but I'm sure she's doing well. Say, what kind of films you been in?"

"I no bee actor, say-nyor. I be Pancho. I ride with Ceesco Keed. We ride in mucho, mucho movies together."

"Right," I said. Was he putting me on?

As I drove along, I noticed that he had taken his gun out of its holster, a real antique, and had began to load and unload bullets into it. I'm not ashamed to say that it made me a little nervous.

"That's quite a gun, " I said, eying it across the seat. Traffic had slowed for a lumbering trash truck. "Is that for real? I mean, have you ever used it?"

"Oh, jess, I using it mucho, mucho times."

"Well, you'd better keep it out of sight," I said. "Don't want the cops to arrest you for carrying a weapon. *¿Me entiendes?*"

"Okay. I put away until we get to Paramount. Ees plenty of time to use it then." I nodded a smile and concentrated on getting past the trash truck. What a nut this guy was!

"Ees make turn to right again, pleez, say-nyor," Pancho said.

I turned at the next corner, Melrose. We were now going back in the direction we'd come. I was going to say something about this when I saw the big arched gate and the Paramount sign coming up on the right. Pancho sure seemed to know his way around.

I pulled up outside the Paramount Gate. There it was, big as life, just like I had seen it in the movies!

Pancho got out, opened up his umbrella, and started into the lot without even saying good-bye.

"Shall I wait for you?" I yelled out sarcastically. "Or shall I pick up you up later?" I was getting pissed off at this guy. No manners, you know what I mean?

As I began to drive off, I noticed the guard at the entrance gate going after Pancho. The Mexican revolutionary was past the guard post and walking across the lot at a fast pace. "Hey, you have to sign in!" I heard the guard call out. Well, I thought, Pancho is your problem now, not mine. And thank God that terrible stench was out of the car!

I consulted the city map cousin Raúl had mailed me and decided to take surface streets: Melrose to Vermont, left on Vermont to Sunset, right on Sunset till it turned into Brooklyn.

My cousin Raúl had a modest law practice handling immigration and naturalization cases. He insisted on living in Boyle Heights, in the same neighborhood as many of his clients.

Although it had been ten years since I had last been in the neighborhood, finding his place wasn't hard. He lived across the street from Prospect Park, right off Brooklyn Avenue, which no longer existed—the name had been changed to César Chávez Avenue in honor of the late farmworker leader.

Other than the changing of the street name, not a whole lot had changed since my last visit. Sure, the graffiti on the walls signaled a new gang in the neighborhood. White Memorial Hospital up the street had added on a couple of new outpatient buildings. But other than that, things looked pretty much as they had before.

I found Raúl washing his car in front of the old Victorian home his parents had bought years ago when they had moved here from Arroyo Grande. Raúl's dad, my uncle Simón, had passed away, but Raúl still lived in the house with his mother, my *tía* Rosita.

"*Cabrón*, you finally made it!" he said, pulling me out of the driver's seat with a big *abrazo*.

"In the flesh," I said returning the embrace.

Boy, it was good to see him! He helped me unload my things and within a few minutes we were sitting in the living room of the ancient house, sipping Tecates and talking about old times.

Raúl explained that my *tía* Rosita was out shopping, but that we'd celebrate with a big dinner as soon as she returned. As I settled into the comfortable living room sofa, Raúl insisted on showing off the latest family acquisition, a large-screen Japanese television set. The screen was three feet across and two and a half feet tall, and the TV had stereo speakers. Boy, we had nothing like this in Arroyo Grande!

My cousin left the TV on but turned down the volume so we could get caught up on old times.

Raúl is a year older than me. He and I had grown up together in Arroyo Grande until I was fifteen. That's when his father decided to move the family to Los Angeles. He had always been my favorite cousin, and as we got to talking, I realized how much I really missed him.

We were into our second beer when my attention was suddenly diverted from Raúl's account of how he had recently won a class-action lawsuit to the TV set he had left on.

"Wait a minute, Raúl," I said.

I jumped up and walked over to the television set. I couldn't believe my eyes! There on the tube was a grainy photo of Pancho, the guy I had dropped off at the Paramount studios only an hour before!

The photo changed to an image of a Chicana news reporter standing in front of the Paramount gate where I had dropped the hitchhiker off. I turned up the volume to hear what she was saying.

"...captured here on security video as he entered the Paramount lot. Witnesses say the deranged assailant, apparently dressed in a rented movie costume, may have had a grudge against the Paramount executive because he shouted something about the films Lawrence Rolling had produced before killing him."

I moved closer to the set. The reporter wasn't bad-looking.

"Police say that before he fled the scene of the crime, the berserk assailant mutilated Rollings' body," the woman continued. "But they have declined to go into specifics. Police believe the suspect may still be on the Paramount lot and are now conducting a building-by-building search."

The scene on the television switched to footage of a wrecked office with blood stains still visible on the pristine white rug.

The reporter's voice-over continued. "Police say this is the first big break they've had in what the press has been labeling the 'movie mogul murders,' five in all including today's killing. In each case the killer has been disguised in a movie costume and has escaped without a trace."

The attractive Chicana returned on camera. "The guard at the Paramount lot described the assailant's accomplice as a male Hispanic, approximately 25 to 30 years of age, dressed in black and wearing a brown fedora."

I gulped.

She went on: "The Paramount guard said the accomplice dropped the killer off here at the studio gate and may have planned to return because he shouted something about picking the suspect up later. The accomplice is presumed to be armed and is believed to be driving a vintage 1950s Black Chevrolet."

I was speechless.

Raúl, who had heard most of the news report, looked out the window to my '49 Fleetline, then back to me, eyeing my black-on-black outfit and the brown fedora on the couch. "Rudy," he asked cautiously, "are you in some kind of trouble?"

Trouble! I had been in Los Angeles for less than a day and was now being hunted for killing a man I had never even met!

"This is all wrong," I said, sitting down. "That guy was a hitchhiker I picked up on my way here. Now I'm a wanted man. Maybe I should go back to Arroyo Grande."

"Not if you're innocent," Raúl said. "Look, I think you should give yourself up, *primo*." Then as an after-thought, "I'll go downtown with you. If you're innocent, we'll be home in time for dinner!"

If I'm innocent? This was my cousin speaking, and even he distrusted me! But he was right. I had to turn myself in. What else could I do?

○ ○ ○

"All right, let's go over it again," the heavyset police investigator said wearily. His name was Thompson. He and his partner, a skinny Black guy named Riggins, were in charge of the police team investigating the movie-mogul murders.

For the past three hours they had been grilling me with questions on the third floor of police headquarters at Parker Center. Giving myself up hadn't been quite the simple solution my cousin had predicted, but at least I hadn't gotten shot. Raúl had gone into Parker Center while I waited, parked in front of the massive glass building in downtown Los Angeles. Within moments, a dozen officers had run out of the building, their guns drawn, and had surrounded the car. I had gotten out carefully with my hands in the air. I had tried to remember everything I had seen on television about how not to provoke police officers into shooting you.

"Look," I insisted to Thompson, "I've already told you everything I know."

"We got bad memories," he said. "Tell us again." He wore a cheap suit with a gun in a shoulder holster, and had a nasty habit of plucking hairs from his nostrils, when he asked questions.

"Okay," I said wearily, "I picked this guy up around La Brea and Santa Monica. He asked me to take him to Paramount Studios. He had on makeup or something. Anyway, his face was all green-colored. And he was wearing this crazy *charro* outfit."

"*Charro* outfit?" Thompson asked.

"Yeah," I replied. "You know, like a Mexican cowboy outfit, the kind *mariachis* wear. Anyway, I dropped him off at the studio and that was it. That's the last I saw of him."

Just then the skinny detective returned. He had gone out a half-hour earlier to check the story I had given them about driving into Los Angeles from Arroyo Grande.

"I just spoke with his friends in Arroyo Grande," Riggins said. "A dozen of them will swear he was doing heavy-duty drinking with them Saturday night, into the wee hours. Also spoke with gas-station attendants in Blythe and Indio. It's just as he says. They remember him because of the car. The guy in Blythe remembers trying to buy it off him."

"That's right," I said, suddenly remembering. "The gas-station attendant *did* make me an offer on the Fleetline."

"That clears him on the other murders as well," Riggins said. "Oh, by the way, the Mayor is waiting to see us."

Thompson and Riggins exchanged very unhappy looks.

"All right," Thompson said reluctantly. "I guess you're cleared. But you'll have to stay in the city until we can arrange for a complete statement in a couple of days."

"Hey, I came to visit my cousin and stay awhile. I'm not going anywhere."

"Oh, and one more thing," Thompson said, showing me to the door. "Keep away from the press for the time being. We don't want to spread any rumors."

Raúl was waiting for me in the lobby, and we finally got back to his house after midnight.

My *tía* Rosita, bless her, had prepared a dinner for us and quickly reheated it as soon as we showed up. We finally had our quiet family dinner at two in the morning.

○ ○ ○

The next morning I was awakened by a pounding on the front door. I look at the clock on the mantle—it was eight in the morning. No wonder my head hurt. Raúl had to be at work by seven, so I figured he was gone by now. I turned over and tried to go back to sleep, figuring my *tía* Rosita would handle the door.

The pounding continued.

I guessed that my *tía* must still have been in bed and I knew I'd never get back to sleep until the pounding went away. So I put on my pants and padded barefoot to the front door. I was still half-asleep and not really thinking very clearly when I opened the door. What a surprise I got! Smiling at me was the most beautiful woman I'd ever seen. I was speechless for a moment, then I remembered. She was the Chicana reporter I had seen on the television report the night before.

What a looker this woman was! High cheekbones, aquiline nose, a smile of perfect white teeth, brown hair that rippled down to her well-endowed breasts, chocolate-colored skin, and intense seductive ebony eyes. She was dressed in a fashionable tan and brown jacket and slacks combination and wore Reebok walking shoes.

"Mr. Vargas?" She asked.

"Huh?" I responded, trying not to gape.

"Are you Mr. Vargas?"

"Yeah..." I said, regaining my wits.

"I'm from Channel 7 News. May I speak with you?"

"Channel 7?"

"I'm a reporter. I've been covering the 'movie-mogul murders.' May I come in?" she asked.

"Yeah," I said, finally back in control of myself. "I mean, sure. Come on in."

I led her into the living room.

"Excuse me a moment," I said, picking up the blankets and pillow off the couch. "Uh, have a seat." I motioned to the couch while I took my "bed" into the adjoining hallway.

I returned to the living room and sat down next to her.

"As I was saying," the reporter said, "I'm doing a story on the studio murders. I understand you picked up one of the…"

"Look, I just got into town," I interrupted. "I don't really know much about these murders. Heck, I hadn't been here more than a half-hour before I picked up that hitchhiker."

A look of understanding spread across her face. "Of course," she said, "that must be why they let you go. You couldn't have been involved in the others, and they know it must be the same person or persons doing the killings."

"Huh?" I said, wishing I could stop sounding so stupid.

"There have been four other murders," she went on. "All within the past week and all the same—film producers, all killed in their office or at home, and all with their eyes gouged out."

"Eyes gouged out?" I gasped. That must have been what she meant by "mutilated" body.

"The cops haven't let out that detail to the press," she continued. "Hollywood is in enough of a panic as it is. I only found out because I saw one of the bodies at the morgue. By the way, my name is María López."

"Pleased to meet you," I said. We shook hands.

"You can call me Rudy," I added. What a gorgeous woman you are, I thought to myself, and smart, too! No ring, but maybe a boyfriend. Yeah, I'm sure of it. With your looks and my luck, probably a dozen.

"I didn't know about the eyes," I said, trying to keep the conversation going. "All four murders?"

"Yes." She nodded seriously. "Now, the hitchhiker you picked up was dressed in a movie costume, right?"

"Right," I said. "And he spoke with a funny accent."

"Exaggerated, would you say?"

"Yeah, how did you know?"

"Fits the M.O.," she said. "In all the other cases, the killer was disguised in a movie costume as well. And in all four, the costumes had to do with some Latin character out of a movie, and each of the killers spoke with a funny Latin accent."

"Then it's the same guy!" I said.

"Not exactly. The first one was an older man dressed as a Mexican peon—you know the kind. The big oversized sombrero, *huaraches*, and white peasant pants and shirt. But the next one was a woman. Eyewitnesses described her as wearing a tight-fitting miniskirt with a beehive hairdoo. They said she looked, and talked, like a prostitute."

"Go on," I said.

"The third and fourth ones were younger Hispanic males, dressed as lowriders," she said.

"Lowriders?" I asked.

"Yes," she said. "Two different killings, but each assailant was dressed in a white t-shirt with khaki pants with a pleat down the front. And each wore a red bandana across the forehead."

"And the fifth was the Mexican revolutionary I picked up," I said, concluding the line-up for her.

"Right," she nodded.

"A regular parade of Hollywood stereotypes," I said.

María paused for a moment and looked at me like I had just said the most profound thing in the world.

"Exactly what I think," she said in a serious tone.

"I don't get it," I said, genuinely puzzled.

"Here, have a look at this." She pulled out several newspaper clippings from her purse and handed them to me.

They were obituaries from the *Los Angeles Times* and something called *The Hollywood Reporter*. I scanned them quickly.

"Notice anything interesting about these guys?" she asked.

"They've all made a lot of movies," I offered. I was trying to figure out what she was driving at.

"But what kind of movies?" she asked pointedly.

Suddenly I saw it. A pattern. The titles of the films jumped out at me: "South of the Border," "Eastside Crime Wave," "Pancho Villa Rides," "Border Kill," "Gangs of East L.A.," "The Return of the Cisco Kid," "Border Brothel." The list was pretty long.

"They all have to do with Mexicans," I said. "Or at least they have Latin themes."

"Exactly," she said, looking straight into my eyes. When she looked at me that way I got butterflies in my stomach.

"Rudy," she whispered, drawing her face up close to mine, "I think there's a connection."

Her lips were so close.

"A connection?" I repeated, mesmerized by her piercing eyes.

"Rudy, it's as if these these guys were being killed by characters out of their own movies."

"Actors that didn't like their parts?" I asked.

"Could be actors," she nodded. "Or someone else."

"But why go through all the trouble to get dressed up as characters out of the movies these guys made?" I asked.

"I don't know," she said. "To make a point, perhaps."

I could see the wheels churning in her pretty little head. "I haven't got it quite figured out yet."

"Look," I said, "I'm just a country boy from Arroyo Grande, Texas. This is all big-city stuff for me. Say, maybe we should have some coffee, huh?"

"Rudy," she persisted, "I know this sounds a little crazy, but I'm serious. There's some connection between the *characters* in the films made by these producers and whoever is killing them. And I don't think it has to do with disgruntled actors."

"I guess it could be most anybody on a film crew, couldn't it?" I asked. I had heard that producers weren't always loved by film crew members.

"Rudy," she said, giving me an intense look. "Don't laugh at me, but what if it isn't actors or crew members? What if there's something...*supernatural* about all of this."

"Supernatural?" I repeated. Oh, no, I thought to myself, she's a nut case. All that beauty and she turns out to have a few marbles loose!

"I have a friend in the police department," she went on. "He tells me that the cops are really freaked out by this one. In two of the cases, security guards claim they emptied their guns at the killer and it didn't even slow him down! Bullets don't seem to have any effect on these guys. And not one of them has been caught; they just seem to disappear into thin air."

At this point I decided that a cup of coffee was definitely in order—for me if not for her. I invited her into the kitchen and made us some instant coffee. I put extra spoonfuls in mine, but had to wait to drink it because the water was so hot.

"Rudy, I'm on the track of the story of the century," she went on, pleading at me with those dark, intense eyes. "I need your help."

Yes, I thought, anything. For those eyes I'd walk to China.

She ignored the cup of coffee I had placed in front of her. "I want you to retrace your steps with me to see if maybe we can't uncover something."

"Sure," I replied to her. "I'd be glad to help." Miss a chance at spending the day with the most attractive woman I had ever met?

"Let's start with the guy you picked up," she went on. "Where exactly was that?"

"Like I told the police," I said, "it was on Santa Monica Boulevard near La Brea."

She pulled a city map out from her purse and spread it out on the kitchen table. There were five red circles on the map, all in the Hollywood area—the site of each of the five murders.

"Look at this," she said, pointing to the map. "Three of the producers were killed at home. One was killed here in the Park La Brea area, another one here in the Hollywood Hills, and the other over here, near Highland and Sunset. A fourth one was killed during a business lunch on the Strip."

Her finger moved across the map. "And you picked up your hitchhiker here at Santa Monica and La Brea. Notice anything interesting about these locations?"

I pored over the map for a moment, trying to figure out what she was getting at. What was I supposed to see? I hated this question-and-answer thing she did. Why couldn't she just say what she meant?

"I don't know what you're getting at," I said finally.

"What I'm getting at is this," she said emphatically, pointing to a green spot on the map adjacent to Santa Monica and La Brea.

I read the fine print. "The Hollywood Memorial Cemetery?" I asked.

"Exactly. Within spitting distance of all five locations. The back of the cemetery borders the Paramount lot. That's how the killer you picked up made his getaway! That's where I think these zombies are coming from," she replied firmly.

"Zombies?" I said, searing my throat with hot coffee.

"Lowrider zombies," she said, giving me that deep, intense, meaningful stare. "That's who's behind all these killings!"

O O O

An hour later I had showered, said goodbye to my *tía* Rosita, and was cruising with María in the Fleetline on the way to the Hollywood Memorial Cemetery.

On the way, I managed to find out that María was a single, career woman and presently unattached. From the frank and encouraging way she was answering my nosy questions, and asking questions about me, I had the feeling she was actually taking a liking to me. Maybe I had a chance!

"The cemetery's got quite a history," she explained on the way. "Lots of famous actors buried there."

"But what's the connection to these lowriders?..." I couldn't bring myself to say it.

"The zombies?" she replied. "I don't quite have that part of the puzzle yet. I'm calling them *lowrider zombies,* but they can be zombies of all kinds, I suppose. They all have one thing in common—they're all Latino characters. At least that's my theory."

"I'm not saying that I'm buying this idea of yours. But, if they are zombies, why are they going after these producers?"

"That's what's got me puzzled," she admitted. "Why does anyone kill another person?"

"Money, love, rejection..." I offered. "Revenge..."

"Revenge!" She savored the word. "That's it! They must be trying to get back at these producers for something, some kind of revenge. That might explain the eyeballs."

"The eyeballs?"

"Blind them? Perhaps its some kind of poetic justice."

"And the cemetery?" I asked.

"Not sure about that. It's got to do with some kind of twisted film logic. I mean, where else would zombies come from—even lowrider zombies—but from a cemetery? You got to think in filmic terms."

"All right," I nodded. "What else do we know about them?"

"Well, they all smell pretty bad, by all accounts," she replied. "And they don't like water."

"Water?" I asked.

"Watch out!" María said suddenly. I had gotten distracted with the conversation and had weaved into the next lane of traffic. I quickly pulled the Fleetline back into my lane and smiled as an angry motorist pulled past us.

"Are you sure about this water thing?" I said, paying more attention to my driving.

She pulled out a worn notepad from her purse and started leafing through it. "Here it is, " María said, reading from her notes. "In the Park La Brea murder the producer's maid walked in on the lowrider just after he had killed her boss. She was carrying a bucket of water, about to mop the room. She was so frightened that she dropped the bucket, splashing water all over the zombie. According to her sworn testimony, he dissolved before her eyes, leaving only the rented costume. The police thought she was in shock, of course, and discounted her testimony."

"Dissolved?" I asked. "Like he melted?"

"That's right," she replied. "I figure it must have been the water that did it. Like the wicked witch of the west in the Wizard of Oz. Remember, think filmic."

"Great," I said. "So we're after the wicked witch of East Los Angeles now."

"Look, I don't know for sure. I'm just speculating. I'm not a zombie expert!"

No, I thought, just working on it.

○ ○ ○

We parked the Fleetwood outside the cemetery on Santa Monica and spent a couple of hours inspecting tombstones, walking down corridors of vaulted urns, and trying not to look too ghoulish to the caretaker who, now and then, crossed our path.

As it turned out, we didn't have anything to worry about. After the third time, we ran into him, we were outside a large mausoleum on the west side of the cemetery, the caretaker stopped us and pointed to the little office at the cemetery entrance.

"They got maps in there," he said. "Save you some time."

"Maps?" I asked.

"Where to find the dead ones, the stars. The map has all the important names and where the gravestones are."

"Oh," I said, getting it. After that I didn't feel so conspicuous. It turns out it was a pretty common thing, traipsing around the Hollywood Cemetery looking at tombstones.

We found nothing having to do with the "mogul murders" and were getting back into the Fleetline when I saw someone coming out of the side entrance to the cemetery. He was dressed like a *bato loco* of the fifties: a black hair net, a cross tattoo on his chin, a genuine Sir Guy shirt, khaki pants, and black French-tipped shoes. A regular *cholo*.

What gave him away was the color of his face. It was the same greenish hue that I noticed on my friend Pancho. And he was carrying a closed umbrella. He had to be one of them.

"Look!" I said to María.

"His face," she said. "It's green."

"Just like I told you," I said. "And look at his umbrella.

"What of it?" she asked.

"Pancho was carrying an umbrella, too. They don't want to take any chances with the rain—meltsville, remember?"

"What's he doing?"

"Looks like he's waiting for a bus," I replied.

Sure enough, the *cholo* was now standing by a bus stop. The people at the bus stop kept their distance from him—the smell, I figured. He didn't have long to wait; within a few minutes a bus pulled up and he got on.

"Let's follow him," María said.

We jumped into the Fleetline and I started off after the bus. For the next hour and a half we tracked our zombie across town. He had boarded the number 4 line going east, toward downtown. We followed a few cars behind the bus, María watching at each stop to make sure he didn't get off. Our *cholo* got off the number 4 at Hill and Sixth Street and then walked over to Broadway where he boarded the number 30 line heading into East Los Angeles.

The number 30 bus traveled up First Street and finally came to a stop at the corner of Mott and First where our zombie got off.

We were in front of the Evergreen Cemetery.

"Visiting relatives?" María quipped.

We got out of the car and watched from a discreet distance as the zombie crossed the street and started toward the cemetery. Then something really strange happened. A couple of local homeboys were walking along the sidewalk with a boombox. The music blaring out of the box was a Ritchie Valens song on an oldies-but-goodies station. It was so loud that María and I could hear it clear across the street. As soon as the homeboys got near our *cholo*, he stopped, grimaced, put his hands to his ears, and started screaming, "No!" He bellowed. "No! Turn it off!" Then he ran screaming head-long into a side gate of the cemetery.

María and I exchanged looks.

I remembered Pancho turning off the car radio
when he had gotten in. "I don't think they like music," I
said.

I explained to María about Pancho and the car
radio.

The two homeboys, meanwhile, looked where the
cholo had run into the cemetery, shrugged their shoulders, and continued on their way. María and I quickly
crossed the street and followed our green *cholo*.

"I'm beginning to feel like Sherlock Holmes," I said
to her.

"Von Helsing might be more like it," she said.

"Von Helsing?" I asked. Where had I heard that
name before?

"Dracula...the guy who goes after Dracula."

Right.

We entered the cemetery at the side entrance but
couldn't see our friend anywhere. I noticed an impressive stone crypt with fancy iron grillwork not far off and
indicated to María that we should check it out. She nodded and started out toward the large stone structure.

We had gone a couple of hundred yards into the
cemetery when suddenly I saw a figure approaching
from the other side of the crypt.

It was Pancho.

"Is that him?" María whispered. He was still dressed
as I had seen him before: the *sombrero*, the *bandoleras*,
and the green face.

"Yes," I whispered back.

Pancho had not seen us and walked straight to the
other side of the crypt. We heard a grating sound and
figured he must have been going inside.

"Come on," María hissed back. "I've got to interview
him!"

On the other side of the crypt we found a metal gate
covering a wooden door. The metal gate slid open easily
enough, but the wooden door wouldn't budge.

"We need a key," I whispered.

I don't know why we were whispering. If María wanted an interview, the best way to get someone out there would be to shout. I guess it was just that the place gave us the creeps.

Suddenly, María pushed hard on the wooden door and it gave way and opened. She smiled and showed me a credit card she held in her hand. "Never fails," she said.

The place was dark and spooky. A couple of feet into the doorway, there was a turn in the small hallway. At the other end of the hallway I saw a door closing behind Pancho.

"Excuse me, sir," María shouted. "Mr. Pancho, may I have a word..." The door slammed shut. We hurried to catch up, but by the time we reached the door we found that it, too, was locked.

María took out her credit card and started in on the door lock. Good looks, brains and initiative, I thought. I was really falling fast for her.

But, damn it, how had I let her talk me into this?

We had just illegally entered someone's crypt. At best this was illegal entry—trespassing. At worst we were committing unholy desecration of the dead!

The more I thought about it the crazier the whole thing seemed. I was about to say something to María when she looked up and saw something behind me.

"Look out!" She shouted.

Then everything went black.

○ ○ ○

It was night when I awoke. I was outside, lying on the grass not far from the crypt. I had a large bruise at the base of my skull and my head ached like hell. María was nowhere to be seen.

I got up and stumbled about the cemetery for a while, but saw no one. I couldn't get the door to the crypt open and really wondered if I wanted to. I didn't know who had clobbered me, but they sure had done a good job.

I was worried about María. Would they have beaten her up? I walked back to the Fleetline and found it locked as we had left it.

Where could she be?

Inside the crypt?

Had she gotten her story and left to file it for the six o'clock news? I could almost believe that. She sure seemed determined to scoop that story. But she wouldn't have left me out there on the grass. Would she?

After a lot of soul-searching and another futile pass through the empty cemetery, I decided to err on the side of safety. *Her* safety. If she was in danger, I wanted to get help to her as fast as possible.

An hour later, I was sitting in the same chair on the third floor of Parker Center trying to convince Detective Thompson and Detective Riggins that I wasn't crazy and that the woman that I had fallen in love with was in the hands of a green *frito bandito* that killed studio executives.

"You expect me to believe that the suspect in the Lawrence Rolling's murder is a zombie?" Thompson asked incredulously.

"*All* the killers have been zombies," I clarified.

I had toyed with the idea of leaving the zombie part out, but somehow I had blurted it out on the second pass of my story. Detective Thompson had been fuming for the past five minutes.

"Not really a zombie in the technical sense," I continued. "I mean they were never real people. They're film zombies; they're characters from films that have come to life. At least that's what María thinks."

"Oh," Thompson said, nodding his head. "You hear that, Riggins? They're not *real* zombies. Why, I'd know a real zombie. That's why we haven't broken the case before. No, they're *movie* zombies. Of course! Why didn't I see it all along?"

He was not a very happy man.

I realized how preposterous it all sounded. And yet, for the first time, I was actually believing in these zombies myself! Heck, how else to explain all that I had seen?

"Let me try it again," I said.

I told Thompson and Riggins how we had spotted the green-faced *cholo* at the Hollywood Memorial Cemetery and how we'd trailed him to the East Side.

I lied about the crypt door, saying we had found it open, but included all the other details including the lump on my head.

"Serves you right," Riggins said smugly. "Trying to grandstand and beat us at our own job, huh?"

Thompson picked another hair out of his nose. "Yeah, and that goes for this Channel 7 dame as well, Marta López."

"María López," I corrected.

"Whatever. She deserves anything she gets!"

"Oh, and there's one other thing," I said, trying to deflect his angry glare.

"Yeah, what's that?"

"I think they don't like music."

"Oh, they don't like music," he said sarcastically. "Well, well. I'm surprised, because I thought all zombies loved music!

"Riggins," he went on, turning red in the face, "is it Mozart or Bach they prefer? Or are they into Elvis?" He was really pissed.

"Look, zombie or not, I've just told you I saw your suspect at the Evergreen Cemetery," I said angrily. "Now, are you going to go down there with me so we can open up that tomb or not?" I was really worried about what might be happening to María.

"Of course we are," Thompson said, relenting. "But for your sake, this had better not be a wild goose chase."

It only took us twenty-five minutes to get to the cemetery, and we found it as abandoned as I had left it.

We found the night watchman, who opened the crypt for us.

The small hallway was as I remember it, but the door at the end of the hallway was open and it only led to a small alcove where there were a dozen urns. There was no trace of María.

"I'm going to ask you once more and you'd better be telling the truth," Thompson said. "You *did* see the suspect here this afternoon?"

"Yes," I said. "It was the same guy, green face and all."

"Well, he's not here now," Detective Riggins said. "Let's get going. It's late and I'm hungry."

"Isn't there anything you can do about María?" I asked. "I mean, can't you put out a missing-persons notice or something?"

Thompson gave me a thoughtful, appraising look. I guess he could tell I was really worried about María.

"Look," Thompson said, giving me his card. "She's gotta be gone twenty-four hours to be missing. If she doesn't turn up in a day or two, you call us. I've put my home number there, just in case. Vargas, I think you're a straight shooter. If you need help give us a call."

After that we got into their car and they dropped me off at the parking lot where I had left the Fleetline.

I sat in the ancient car and listened to the radio for a while. I tried to get my thoughts in order.

After the third traffic report of a tie-up on the Santa Monica freeway and the second weather report informing me that it was going to rain all day tomorrow and then be sunny for a week, I decided to turn the radio off. My mind was a jumble, but I had to do some serious thinking.

What did I know?

That stereotype film zombies were killing Hollywood producers. That they dissolved if you threw water on them. That they hated music. Or at least some kinds of music—Thompson's wise crack about Mozart had actually given me an idea. Maybe it wasn't all music they hated, but some kinds of music.

Think filmic, I kept saying to myself.

I also knew that they probably had María and that she was probably in danger. I kept coming back to the cemetery—it all had something to do with the cemetery. But there hadn't been anyone at the cemetery. Think filmic.

Then it struck me...midnight! In horror movies things always happen at midnight in the cemetery. I looked at my watch: it was eleven-thirty. I started the Fleetline and headed out.

O O O

It was beginning to sprinkle by the time I got to the cemetery. The gate was locked, so I jumped over the fence. I was hoping I wouldn't run into the night watchman. He had been pretty pissed off about being disturbed when Thompson had dragged him away from his favorite television show.

It took me a moment to get my bearings in the dark, but then I saw the silver glint of rain splashing off the crypt that we had entered. I was about to set out for it when I saw a figure coming out from the other side. It was dark and the figure was huddled, trying to keep dry. I couldn't make out who it was, but I wasn't going to take any chances on another conk on the head.

I hid behind a tall marble obelisk and raised the flashlight I held in my hand. If anyone was going to get it this time, it wasn't going to me.

The figure passed by me, and I was just about to creep up and hit him from behind when he was illuminated by the light from a nearby streetlamp. It was María!

"María!" I yelled. I ran up to her and took her in my arms.

"Oh, Rudy," she said, falling into my embrace. Suddenly she was kissing me and I was kissing her. We held on to each other for a long time, the rain really beginning to come down and both of us ignoring it.

"Where have you been?" I finally managed to say. "I've been worried sick about you. Are you all right?"

"I'm fine," she said excitedly. "I've been hiding out under that crypt all afternoon."

"Hiding out? What happened?" I asked.

"You were clobbered by that *cholo* we were following," she said. "When he hit you, I tried to run past him, but tripped and fell. My head must have hit something because I was out for a moment. But when I came to, I saw the *cholo* entering the room behind the locked door—it's some kind of vault for funeral urns."

"Right, I've seen it," I said. I explained to her about bringing the police to search for her.

"Oh, Rudy," she said, "I knew you were a special kind of guy." She kissed me again, long and passionately. God, I really did have a chance with her!

"There's a secret doorway that leads down a long flight of steps deep into the ground," María said.

Of course, I thought, think filmic. Crypts in horror movies always have secret passages.

"Rudy, this story is even bigger than I thought!" she said. "Under that crypt there's a huge vault, and there are several hundred of these zombies gathered down there. They were having some kind of meeting when I got there."

"Regular zombie jamboree, eh," I said grimly.

"They were talking about their plan to attack."

"Attack?" I asked.

María gave me that serious, I-mean-business nod. "Rudy," María said, "these studio murders are just the beginning!"

"The beginning of what?"

"The end of civilization. They're planning mass murders!"

"What are you talking about?"

"They're all down there, hundreds of them, lowriders, prostitutes, drug dealers, bandits, gang members, Latin lovers, Mexican spitfires—every stereotype you can think of, and they're planning to come up and attack the world."

"But I thought they were just after Hollywood executives..." I began.

"Not anymore," María said. "At first it was studios, producers, writers, directors, but now they're after everyone—even people who've never even made films about Latinos. They've gone beserk and they're going to start their attack as soon as this rain clears up."

"But why?" I asked incredulously.

"It has something to do with the freeing of their souls," María replied. "At least that's what I heard one of them say."

"Freeing their souls?" I said. Zombies with souls? This was getting weirder and weirder.

"That was this afternoon," she continued. "When I started to go back, I got lost in the dark and couldn't find the steps leading back up here. So I hid in a funeral niche all evening trying not to be discovered. Then a little while ago one of them them started back up the steps and I followed him out."

"Well, let's get out of here," I said, pulling her in the direction of the cemetery wall. "I've seen all I want of these zombies or whatever they are."

"Rudy," María said as we neared the cemetery wall, "we've got to do something. We've got to tell the police and warn people."

"I know," I said.

I had been doing a lot thinking as María told me her story. And then I began to piece together other things that I had overlooked. Pancho turning off the radio when he got into the car. And the *cholo* running from the homeboys. I remembered the songs that had been playing. I began to formulate a plan—a plan that just might work.

"Come on," I said, "I gotta call my pal, Detective Thompson."

"Good," she said. "The police need to be notified, then we can come back for the footage."

"Footage?" I asked incredulously. "You want to go back there?"

"That's why I came up, to get the videocam I left in your car. The station'll need footage with my report. I'll show you how to operate the camera while I do the stand-up. Think of it, reporting from a secret zombie hideout. What a scoop!"

This was nuts. "María..." I began.

"Rudy, I can't very well bring an entire news crew out here. We'll just have to make do, you and me. The videocam has a built-in mike and a spotlight. It's easy to operate."

"All right," I said, "but first let's make that phone call."

I knew what I had to do and exactly how to do it. I fished Detective Thompson's card out of my pocket, found a phone booth, and made the call. He was as angry at being wakened from his sleep and as unbelieving as ever at first. But then he quieted down and listened.

There had been yet another murder earlier that evening, this time on the Disney lot, and Detective Thompson was ready to grasp at straws.

I told him that evacuating East Los Angeles was the first step. María had confirmed that, in their deranged state, the zombies would go after anyone who got in their way. We had twenty-four hours. I was sure the zombies wouldn't make a move as long as it was raining.

I suggested to Thompson that the L.A. River would be a good place to make a stand. They'd have to come across on the First, Fourth, or Seventh Street bridges to get to Hollywood, and we could set up my plan there.

He didn't even say my idea was ridiculous and stupid, he just kept asking me to slow down so he could take down the very specific instructions I gave him.

By the time I was finished with the phone call, María had loaded a cassette in the videocam. She quickly showed me how to turn the thing off and on, and then we set out to videotape our dear friends.

We got back into the crypt easily enough and found the steps. But when we reached the bottom, I thought I was going to pass out, the stench was so unbearable!

In the dimly lit vault, I could make out hundreds of zombies. They were all standing still, their mouths gaping open and eyes closed, like they were in some kind of heavy sleep. But their faces were contorted in pain. If they really were characters out of movies, it would be the pain of hundreds of films' worth of moral and psychological abuse. No wonder they were in pain.

"Let's get your footage and get out of here," I whispered.

I managed to frame a nice shot of María with the zombies in the background for her on-camera introduction. I turned on the light and she started her story. She had spoken for a good five minutes and I had gotten quite a lot of pan shots of the zombies, when suddenly they started waking up.

They spotted us and all hell broke loose!

In a moment we were running for our lives. We managed to make it back to the steps, but a group of zombies had gotten there before us and were blocking the doorway at the top.

Fortunately, they didn't see us. I spotted a maintenance closet nearby, grabbed María, and ducked in.

We spent the next day in the closet, trying not to make noise and hoping our bladders would hold out until we could get away.

All during the day we heard the distant sound of helicopters and the muffled blare of loudspeakers. We felt the rumble of traffic passing on nearby First Street.

I figured the evacuation must have been underway.
Finally, at dawn the next day, when neither María nor I
could hold it any longer, we crept out of the closet and
worked our way up the steps. We were in luck: there
was no one around. We made our getaway.

We finally relieved ourselves in the bushes of the
cemetery and were coming out of the cemetery grounds
when we saw that the entire block was surrounded by
zombies. It was a beautiful morning: the rain had
stopped, the sun was shining, and there wasn't a cloud
in the sky.

The zombies had started their attack. Everywhere
we looked we could see bands of zombies turning over
cars and setting fire to buildings as they made their way
westward to Hollywood.

Our salvation was the '49 Fleetline. It was where I
had left it, and María and I wasted no time in jumping
in and heading toward downtown.

"I'll marry you if we get through this alive," María
said as I careened the car down First Street.

"Sure thing," I replied. "We'll have the fanciest wedding Arroyo Grande's ever seen."

"You mean Los Angeles!" she said firmly.

We made it past Boyle and down the hill on First
Street, and then continued past the Aliso Village housing project. I could see that the police had already been
through here. There wasn't a soul in sight. Ahead we
could see the First Street Bridge. At the crest of the
bridge, where it arched over the Los Angeles River, was
a police barricade with a squadron of police cars, ambu-
lances, and television news trucks. It looked like all of
Los Angeles had turned out to witness the army of
destruction that was closing in behind us.

I drove the Fleetline to the crest of the bridge and
we got out. Our location gave us a commanding view of
the East Los Angeles horizon, and quite an eerie sight it
was. As far as we could see there were fires raging; there

must have been a thousand plumes of smoke billowing into the sky.

"Hey, you two, get over here!"

I turned and saw Detective Thompson coming toward us. As he got closer and recognized me, he let out a slow whistle. "I thought we'd lost you, Vargas." He recognized María. "Glad to see you, too, Ms. López."

"Did you set it up?" I asked.

"Yeah, and not any too soon," he said. "Look."

He pointed over our shoulders where we could see the army of movie stereotypes starting up the First Street Bridge.

What a truly gruesome sight it was: bandits, lowriders, prostitutes, *mamasitas*, peons and wetbacks— beings distorted beyond recognition into cruel, sniveling, disgusting caricatures of humanity.

I could begin to make out what they were saying.

"Hey, meester, I sell you my seester, yes?"

"Oh, you gringos very smart!"

"Hey, dude, you wanna score some heroin?"

"He went that-a-away, meester."

"I need my migra papers!"

It was the cruel, senseless babble of a hundred racist movies.

We quickly made our way back to the police barricade. I looked up and saw that, true to his word, Thompson had set up an array of large speakers all along the metal infrastructure of the First Street Bridge.

The lowrider zombies were closing in on us now. There was hatred in their eyes, the pent-up hatred of hundreds of tasteless, demeaning lines, hundreds of sick, denigrating images. "*¡Ojos!*" they started chanting. "We want eyeballs!"

What they wanted, I thought to myself, was their humanity back. But I knew neither I nor anyone on that bridge could give them that. Maybe we couldn't give them back their humanity, but maybe I could put them out of their misery. And that is exactly what I hoped my plan would do. Put these poor bastards out of their misery forever.

As they got closer, Detective Thompson got on his walkie-talkie and started giving orders.

"Wait till they reach the center of the bridge," he said, "then let them have it."

"I sure hope this works," he said to me.

So did I.

I had gotten the idea when I remembered what had been playing on my radio when the hitchhiking *frito bandito* had gotten in my '49 Fleetline. An original version of the same song, popular in the fifties, had been playing on the homeboy's boombox, and that's what had driven our gangbanger crazy. Now I was hoping it would work the same magic here.

"Let 'em have it," Thompson said over the walkie-talkie.

Then the music started.

I drew María close to me. We were at the west end of the bridge now, behind the police barricade. We were about to witness the most eerie battle in human history.

I knew that María's reporting career would be made tonight. With the story she had uncovered and the exclusive footage we'd gotten of the zombies in their underground lair, she'd win an Emmy for sure.

I also knew that she had been kidding about getting married in Los Angeles because we'd already discussed that. We had agreed to get married in Arroyo Grande. We'd discussed a lot of things while we were stuck for a day in that closet in the crypt.

"Listen," María said, clutching my arm.

The strains of music were now filtering down from the high structure of the bridge to street level where the zombies were attacking. The music caught them in the middle of the bridge and one by one they began to drop to the ground. They squirmed and writhed on the ground, holding their ears and screaming in agony.

"No, no!" shrieked an anguished Mexican bandit.

"Anything but that!" howled a berserk Latin lover.

"Turn it off!" screamed a crazed Cuban fireball.

My plan was working. Slowly a cloud of steam began to rise from the street. They were dissolving before our very eyes, as if someone had thrown water on them.

A few tried to flee from the music by jumping over the bridge, only to find that Detective Thompson had diverted water into the usually empty Los Angeles riverbed.

It was ghastly sight.

"Louder," shouted Thompson into the walkie-talkie. "Turn up the volume!"

The familiar and unmistakable song that had bounced around the barrio for a hundred years before it had been made into a movie echoed off the metal infrastructure of the bridge. The song, once a popular dance tune of the Mexican people, had over the years become its own stereotype, a signature song that had become so popularly identified with Latinos that, like the zombies, had become a stereotype itself.

And that's why the song was destroying the zombies. It was the ultimate in fighting fire with fire. Only this ultimate of stereotypic songs could put these anguished zombies out of their misery.

"No," they screamed in agony, "anything but that!"

It was the familiar lyrics I had heard a million times in my life.

"*...Yo no soy marinero, por ti seré, por ti seré.*
Bamba, Bamba, Bamba, Bamba..."

The music and lyrics of *La Bamba* settled over the First Street Bridge as the last of the lowrider zombies melted and dissolved into the air.

The Great Pyramid
of Aztlán

The Great Pyramid of Aztlán

The plane banked away from the sun and swept over the foothills west of Tucson on its final approach to the airport. From my window seat, I looked out over the arid landscape and winced. It was going to be damn hot down there.

The angle of the plane's descent caused the sun to reflect off swimming pools in a well-to-do housing development. As the light played on their mirrored surfaces, the pools glistened and sparkled like tiny gems in a grand baroque design. Not far off, the desert floor rolled out to the horizon like an unfolding rug sprinkled with toy cacti. As the plane banked again, the Catalina mountains came into view, looking like granite skyscrapers that framed the city's flat desert architecture.

With the banking of the plane, the fountain pen I had salvaged from Mrs. Romero's sinkhole as a cub reporter years ago rolled off the seat tray on which I had been writing and onto the floor. I picked it up and looked at it for a moment. Over the years it had become a bit of a lucky charm for me. I had used it on prize-winning news assignments, to sign my contract with the *Los Angeles Times,* and even to fill out the marriage form when Gloria and I had gotten hitched. I had replaced the ink cartridge only once, and yet here it was once again accompanying me on another assignment for the paper. And what an assignment this was going to be.

A bell sounded and the fasten-seat-belt light came on. I put my pen and papers away and adjusted the back of my seat forward. As the plane landed and taxied to the terminal, I considered again the preposterous notion that brought me there from Los Angeles. It still seemed unbelievable: the building of a giant pyramid in the middle of the Arizona desert?

Two days earlier, the city editor, Samuel Samuels (God's truth), called me into his office. As I entered, I knew it couldn't be good news. I'd seen that grim-faced, father-why-hast-thou-forsaken-me-look before.

"Frank, I got a problem," he said, avoiding eye contact. "I need someone to cover a human-interest story in Arizona." He handed me a *Newsweek* clipping.

"You're the man for it," he said.

Without looking at the clipping, I said, "What? Another Mexican story?"

It iced him. I knew it would.

"Now, Frank, let's not get into that again," he said. "Look, if it were a math story and you were a math expert, I'd send you. And you wouldn't complain. Let's face it: you're an expert. Live with it! Your beat just happens to be..." He left it unfinished.

I scanned the article. It was about a group of Chicanos who were building a giant pyramid in their ancestral homeland, Aztlán. Another Chicano story—another assignment for Frank del Roble. God, I hate being pigeonholed!

Now, don't get me wrong, it's not like I wasn't qualified. I'd been through those picket lines and riots of the '60's with the best of them. Hell, I took great pride in my photo collection: César Chávez with an arm around my shoulder; an autographed photo of Bobby Kennedy. And the other ones. Photos of me with Anthony Quinn, Lee Treviño, Ricardo Montalbán. That had been when I was a cub reporter in Arroyo Grande, Texas. Later, when I got the *Los Angeles Times* job, it was photos of me with Mayor Henry Cisneros, Mayor Federico Peña, Supervisor Gloria Molina, and on and on.

Yes, I guess I *was* an expert of sorts. And who better to handle a story about Chicanos building a pyramid in the desert? I was Spanish-surnamed, bilingual, I had an affinity for the subject matter, and, of course, I had a lot of community contacts in Tucson. The story fit me like a glove.

A well-worn glove.

Looking up from the clipping, I knew I would have to take the assignment. But, I thought, not without some consciousness-raising on old Samuels.

"You're stereotyping me again," I said. "All I get sent out on are these Chicano stories. It's limiting my potential as a reporter. Why don't you send me on a story to D.C. or New York? The White House, the United Nations, Wall Street...Why don't you let me write about something like that?"

His reply was the same as always: something about the location of the office exit and my ambulatory options if I didn't like the assignment—with, of course, the accompanying monetary repercussions. Of course, I took the assignment. I may have been born Mexican, but not yesterday. And, after all, Gloria gets *so* touchy when I'm on unemployment.

And so, Tucson again.

○ ○ ○

It took me a half-hour to dig my luggage out of the baggage claim area, and another half-hour to rent a car and drive out to the Sunburst Motel. "Economical," Samuels had said. "Keep it economical." Well, the Sunburst sure fit the bill.

As I threw my overnight bag and briefcase on the dusty bed and looked out the window to the gravel parking lot, the place struck me as being much seedier than I remembered from previous visits. But then, most of those stopovers had occurred when I was covering Chicano-Movement stories for the *Arroyo Daily Times*. It was a time in my career when I was thankful to stay any place other than someone's living room floor. I guess

my healthy expense account at the *Los Angeles Times*
had spoiled me.

After a dip in the Sunburst's pool, I settled down in
my room with a couple of beers with ice. I started in on
the my phone calls I'd need for the story.

According to the *Newsweek* piece (a muckraking item
on how government money was being misspent), an
enterprising Chicano named Manuel Zapata had
received some kind of federal grant to build a pyramid,
each of whose sides was to be a mile long. I tried to imagine how tall that would make the pyramid itself. A half a
mile? Three-quarters of a mile? Wouldn't something that
big just cave in on itself? Evidently not. Someone seemed
to be building it.

My first job was to follow through with the reporters' maxim you learn the first term in journalism
school: call who you know.

Solomón Barragán, a long-time Tucson activist and
good friend, was surprised to hear from me after so
many years. When I told him I was in town, he became
elated. When I told him *why* I was in town, he exploded.

"Of course, I know about the pyramid," he said. "I'm
working there! And my *carnal*, Armando, he's in charge
of the construction."

And that's why maxims are maxims.

○ ○ ○

Solomón picked me up the next morning at nine.
After a warm *abrazo*, we began our traditional barrage
of mutual insults. He zeroed in on my expansive beer
belly and I rejoined with attacks on his receding hair-
line. Truth to tell, however, forty had been much kinder
to Solomón than it had been to me.

"Come on, let's go," he said, motioning me to a shiny
Bronco XLT. I remembered the battered blue VW that
Solomón had been driving the last time I came through

town. The pyramid was evidently doing good for some people.

On the way to the pyramid, I had a chance to catch up on Solomón's activities since the summer three years ago when I had covered his abortive bid for City Council. He told me that recently he had spearheaded a nasty fight with City Hall over swimming-pool rights for Chicano kids.

"That kind of stuff still happens," he said, giving me an exasperated look that conveyed more than his words. We talked about his romance with Marta that had gone full route in my absence. I congratulated him on the marriage, but avoided his queries about Teresa, the local Tucsonian whom I had not seen in many years. Even after I had married Gloria, I was still recovering from whiplash of the heart over *that* one.

"But the big news is the *pirámide*," he said. He pronounced it in Spanish, pee-ráh-me-deh. "That's where the action is now!"

We drove through Tucson on a four-lane highway someone had name Oracle Road. I suppose retaining the name even after the two-lane wagon trail had become a four-lane highway was the city father's idea of keeping Tucson small. No-growth philosophy at its best.

Soon we moved out of the city and the four-lanes became a well-traveled two-lane highway. We were out in the desert.

Within a short while, traffic began to slow as we came up behind a caravan of large trucks filled with construction materials. I could see cement bags, lumber, and metal beams.

"I wouldn't think there'd be so much traffic out here in the desert," I said.

Solomón looked over to me as if I had said something really dumb. "You can build a pyramid without construction materials?" he asked. I looked at the trucks ahead of us and realized what he meant.

"All of them?" I asked.

"All of them," he said. "Here, I'll take a back route."

With a swirl of the steering wheel, he spun the Bronco off the highway and took us careening across the desert. We bounced between saguaro and prickly pear and, within a few minutes, found what looked to me like a cowpath. Solomón assured me it was "the back road." The Bronco settled into a rhythmical bouncing. Soon the rolling Sonoran terrain ahead gave way to a rise in the road, which appeared to end somewhere off in the distant horizon.

What I took to be an abandoned car at the crest of the horizon line began to grow in size as we approached. After a while, I realized that it wasn't a car at all. It was some kind of structure, irregularly shaped, with portions jutting into the sky.

As we got closer, I began to fidget in my seat. "*¡Chingao!*" I exclaimed. "That thing is immense!"

Solomón was beaming.

"*¡Puesluégole!*" he replied, as if stating the obvious. "As long as you're going to build one, might as well make it the biggest and best in the world. No?"

I couldn't argue with that.

The closer we got, the larger the pyramid grew. After about a half-hour of driving, we were still quite a distance from the monument. I began to discern movement at its base. It took another few minutes for it to sink in to me that the dots that flickered along the pyramid base were, in fact, men.

"My God!" I said, "it's enormous!"

Solomón nodded, not even looking in my direction.

It was truly a man-made mountain, reminding me of the accomplishment of Teotihuacán.

Finally, we reached the main gate at the barbed-wire fence that surrounded the pyramid site. In the background, a cement wall rose hundreds of feet into the air. I was flabbergasted. As we waited in line behind other traffic, I noted that the barbed-wire fence stretched as far as I could see in both directions. Evidently, it ran the perimeter of the pyramid.

"Now *that* must have cost some bread, eh?" I said, pointing to the fence.

"Not really, " said Solomón. "It was donated."

"By whom?" I asked, taking out my reporter's notebook and beginning to jot down notes with that trusted pen. I was on the clock now.

"The I.N.S.," he said matter-of-factly.

He was waiting for me to bite and what else could I do? "Okay, why did the Immigration and Naturalization Service of the United States of America donate the barbed-wire fence?"

Solomón's smile widened. He knew he had me and reveled in it.

"When we first started work on the *pirámide*, we had a lot of *ilegales* working here," Solomón continued. "The folks in Tucson didn't like all of these people from across the border filtering down to Tucson on weekends. So they raised quite a protest."

The Bronco inched slowly along in traffic. "Well," Solomón went on, "as you can imagine, this led to I.N.S. raids on the *pirámide*. Of course, all that meant was that the *ilegales* would be deported to Nogales one day and they'd be back to work on the *pirámide* the very next day. Finally, someone wised up. The I.N.S. officials decided to look the other way. They'd let the *ilegales*, or as we say here, 'undocumented workers,' work on the *pirámide* as long as they stayed on the grounds during the weekends."

Solomón nodded to the sturdy chain link. "They built the fence to keep the 'illegal' Mexicans *in*. Of course, for us, the fence also works to keep tourists and other undesirables out. It works both ways. We think of it as our tax dollars at work."

By now we were at the sentry gate. Solomón drove the four-wheel past a teenage boy wearing a "Pyramid Power" t-shirt. The young man waved us on. "Student workers," Solomón explained in answer to my questioning nod.

"We got a federal subsidy to hire students from Arizona State University the first year of the *pirámide*. The students were a little snooty and stuck-up at first. They acted as if working on a *pirámide* was below their station in life. *¿Me entiendes?*"

I nodded understanding. My life was full of run-ins with such assholes.

"We soon turned them around. In fact, several of our top engineers are graduate students from the university who decided to stay on. Most of the students are good people at heart. They get over the university experience as soon as they meet real people. Hell, the students we have working with us now have a lot of soul. A lot of them are Chicanos, and those that are not act like they are!"

The four-wheel rose over a gentle hill on a much used road. Below us a valley came into view. Solomón stopped the Bronco and allowed me to take in the vista. It was mighty impressive. To the right, at the end of the dirt road, the pyramid foundation began. Made of stone blocks, each about ten feet tall, the foundation stretched as far as the eye could see.

The walls of the pyramid were covered with cement, giving it a smooth, monolithic look. I realized that part of the visual impact was due to an optical illusion. By seeing the pyramid foundation from this vantage point, at the apex of one corner, the pyramid sides appeared to go off into infinity in each direction.

I could see that construction was at different stages of completion. I noted that, here and there, portals led into the pyramid's interior, which was honeycombed with tunnels and passages. Workmen went in and out with the regularity and single-mindedness of ants at an anthill. I looked to the topmost section of the construction, fully thirty stories high.

"My God, Solomón," I said. "This is amazing! How did you ever get so far in the construction? Who designed this damn thing? And why? Why, above all, is anyone building this crazy thing?"

Solomón turned to me. "I'll let Zapata tell you all about it," he said. "Come on, let's see if we can find him." With that, he started the Bronco up again and we drove to a group of low-roofed cottages adjacent to the nearest pyramid wall.

As we got out of the Bronco, I was nearly felled by a team of construction workers carrying a large I-beam on their shoulders. Solomón pushed me aside in time to avoid my decapitation.

"¡Cuidado!" one of the men yelled angrily.

He was angry! Before I could answer with an appropriate expletive, one of the other men echoed his complaint.

"Watch where you're going, *ése!*" he yelled indignantly. Then he stopped for a moment and looked me over real carefully.

"Frank? Frank del Roble?" he asked.

I looked at him and realized he looked really familiar. Damn if it wasn't Bobby Hernández from Arroyo Grande!

"Bobby Hernández, is that you?"

"Sure is! What the heck are you doing out here?" he asked as he took a breather.

"Doing a story for the newspaper. But what about you? Last time I remember, you had graduated from Arroyo Grande high and were joining the army."

"That I did. Got out and I've been here for three years. But I'm not the only one from back home. Remember the Sluggers? Well, Robert and Johnnie Rodríguez are here and so is Jeanie de la Cruz. And even Rudy 'Bugs' Vargas is working here. Hey, got to get back to work."

He turned to Solomón. "Why don't you take him down to the Tláloc, and I'll catch up with you guys at quitting time." He waved and was gone.

We walked on, my mind still absorbing the fact that there were people from my home town working on the pyramid. We approached one of the buildings in the cottage complex and I stopped to take in an elaborate billboard overlooking the office buildings. The sign read: THE GREAT PYRAMID OF AZTLÁN. *Lo que el viento se llevó, el viento devolvió.* Someone with a great deal of artistic ability had designed an impressive logo for the pyramid and had tagged on the epigram: *What the wind blew away, the wind has returned.*

I was truly impressed with the artwork. It wasn't the usual *rascuachi*, amateurish artwork I had come to associate with so many Chicano projects. No, this was legit, professional, high tech. What *was* this pyramid all about?

We walked into the office and Solomón directed me to a table where a short man with distinctive Indian features sat busily working at a computer terminal. Solomón tapped the man on the shoulder, noticeably startling him.

"Manuel Zapata," Solomón said, "this is Frank del Roble. He's one of our great Chicano reporters from Los Angeles. He's the guy doing the story on us."

Zapata rose from his desk, and I saw that he was even shorter than I had thought. His expression was mean. Straight black hair fell across his forehead and partially obscured his intense eyes. He had an emphatic (how else to describe it?) *zapatista* mustache. I could tell he didn't like being disturbed. He said nothing as he looked me over with—reporter's license—cruel, penetrating eyes.

I became nervous. I smiled weakly and then offered my hand. "My friends call me Frank," I said.

Zapata looked to Solomón. Then he reluctantly extended his hand to me in the traditional La Raza handshake—a test of manual dexterity invented during the heyday of the Chicano-power movement.

I was halfway through the ritual before I realized that he was improvising some variation of his own. I felt foolish trying to keep up with what were obviously well-practiced hand routines unknown to me. Finally, my grasp of his hand slipped and I was left with my hand outstretched in the air as he completed the sacred ceremony by himself.

He looked up to me with a sneer reminiscent of something I had seen on a late-night movie about Nazis. Then he looked to Solomón as if he had just proved a point.

Boy, had I had blown it! A reporter, no matter how good, is going to make mistakes, *faux pas*, social blunders from time to time. But looking like a fool is not the best way to get the story you're after. I knew that at this moment my whole credibility was on the line. Getting the story I was sent to get depended on Solomón pulling me out of this one. I looked to him pleadingly. I wanted him to say something that would make everything all right.

Instead, Solomón nodded to Zapata and said, "Real *pendejo*, eh?" and then proceeded to break out in hearty laughter.

Zapata immediately followed suit. And me? What else could I do? I laughed right along with them, not very happy at why we were laughing.

"It's a test," a transformed, now-smiling-and-friendly Zapata said to me. "I do it all the time. It's a way of telling who are the *pendejos* and who the snakes are." I wasn't sure whether or not I had passed, nor in which category I fell.

"Mr. Zapata," I began again, "Solomón said you could fill me in on the story behind the pyramid. How it got started and things like that."

"Sure," Zapata said, still smiling. "Come on," he continued with a wave of his hand. "I'll give you the royal tour. The one we give the *gringo* investors."

With that, we were off again in the Bronco. Solomón directed the four-wheel down a winding road that ran parallel to the nearest pyramid wall. I took in the incredible size again. A mile on each side? That can't be, I reasoned with myself. Perhaps it could.

"I began the project several years ago with a foundation grant," Zapata began proudly.

"Which one?" I asked, once again taking out my notebook.

"Which one? But there's only one foundation," he replied pointing to the pyramid.

"No," I said, "I mean which foundation gave you the money?"

"Oh," he said realizing my point. "It was actually a joint venture. Ford and Rockefeller put up the initial grant. That is, they put up the money to build the foundation of the *pirámide*.

"Wait a minute," I said drawing back. "The Ford and Rockefeller Foundations gave you a foundation grant? I mean, they gave you a grant to *build* a foundation?"

"Of course," he said with a twinkle in his eye. "Isn't that what foundation grants are for?"

"Of course," I agreed, not sure if he was putting me on, but not wanting to appear stupid.

He went on. "I submitted a proposal for a fellowship to study and recreate the basic plan of the *Teotihuacán pirámide*. You know, I wanted to go back to my indigenous roots—our ancestors knew quite a lot, you know."

I nodded vague understanding.

"So," he went on, "I got a combined grant to build a modest, table-sized model of the foundation of the *Teotihuacán pirámide*. I guess they figured it would look good on the cover of one of their annual reports."

"But this?" I said, motioning to a group of men busily laying in one of the ten-foot stone squares.

"That came much later," he continued. "After I got the grant for the design and construction of what we were then calling the *pirámide,* I got another grant to

build an even larger model, about twenty feet tall. I figured if nothing else, I could convert it into a backyard
slide for my kids. Well, as luck would have it, my secre-
tary is not too good of a speller. Instead of spelling it
"model," she spelled it "motel."

"Motel?" I asked.

"Yep, throughout the whole proposal."

"Well, we didn't get the grant," he continued. He
spoke with the seasoned pace of someone used to telling
this story many times.

"Ford and Rockefeller said it was out of their funding guidelines. But a Chicano program officer at Rockefeller sent the proposal over to someone he knew at the
federal level. A week later I got a call from a guy at the
Department of Housing and Urban Development. He
wanted to talk to me about a minority-owned motel
franchise, built in the shape of a pyramid. That was the
first serious money we got."

By now the four-wheel was passing by a part of the
pyramid wall where construction had evidently been
completed. The smooth cement finish had been painted
over in the bright colors of a mural painting depicting
the life of early indigenous people of the Valley of Mexico. Drawing heavily from the works of Rivera, Siquei-
ros, Orozco, and other Mexican masters, the murals also
had their share of Almaraz, Baca, Botello, Malaquías,
Gronk, Healey, and Magu influences. It was encouraging to see brown faces staring back at me from the pyramid walls. Chicano art appeared to be alive and well in
the Arizona desert.

"We were halfway through the building of what we
thought would be a twenty-unit motel," Zapata went on,
"when someone in Tucson wrote a newspaper article on
us. Overnight we became famous—at least locally. Within
a month we had a million-dollar loan from the SBA,
Small Business Administration. That's about when the
Labor Department got involved."

"The U.S. Department of Labor?" I asked, writing quickly in my notebook.

"Right. This guy, a Puerto Rican brother, was working in the Department of Labor and his job was to develop projects that employed minorities. He said if I wrote up a proposal to them, I might be able to get the Department of Labor to subsidize the hiring of full-time construction workers."

"I was reluctant at first," Zapata confided. "Hell, I said, enough is enough! But this guy said that the previous year they hadn't used up all their funding. If their funds were not fully committed this year, Congress would likely cut them back. He might lose his job. I felt sorry for the guy. So I applied. Damn if we didn't get an award for two million eight! The twenty units became sixty!"

By now we had taken a side road off the main road that ran by the pyramid wall. I thought for a moment we might be going off into the desert again, but the road led to a hilltop instead. Solomón parked the Bronco and we got out. From here we had a commanding view of the entire pyramid project.

Zapata pointed with pride to the far end of the pyramid structure where I could see that work had progressed even more.

"We get our stone brought in by train," he explained. "That's why that side is almost finished. We worked on it first, since it's closer to the railroad tracks."

I looked to where he pointed and could already imagine the inward and upward angling that would eventually result in the classic tetrahedral shape. I followed the slope of the wall and continued an imaginary line to a point just below some cumulus clouds overhead.

"About that time the investors came onto the scene," Zapata said, interrupting my reverie.

"Investors?"

"*Sí, señor*," he said, motioning me to follow him to another vantage point on the hilltop.

"Investors, and lots of them. It started with U.S. firms. I think McDonald's was the first. They wanted to set up golden arches outside the pyramid motel. Before we could even sign the deal, Hilton and Sheraton were vying for a co-venture hotel franchise. They felt the pyramid was the ideal flagship for their revamped hotel chain. We settled for Hilton, with the McDonald's franchise inside the *pirámide*. Then we let in other companies: Kentucky Fried Chicken, Pizza Hut, and Pollo Loco."

"By now we were *the* Hispanic business enterprise," Zapata continued proudly. "We were featured on the cover of *Hispanic Business* magazine. Of course, the more companies that jumped into the fray, the bigger and more complicated the *pirámide* got. By the time the Japanese came into the project, we were looking at a *pirámide* that was a quarter of a mile on each side and thirty stories high. We figured it would cost upwards of thirty million dollars."

"It was then," he went on, "that we had to get the Hispanic politicians involved. Because of protectionist policies, we had to get special legislation passed to allow the heavy Japanese and German investments."

At this point, Zapata was straining my credibility. The pyramid, I could buy, but the idea of Hispanic politicians having enough clout to pass any legislation on the Hill sounded far-fetched. I put the question to my now dust-covered host.

"It's simple," Zapata answered. "Sure, Hispanic congressmen and senators can't make much headway getting worthy programs like day-care, bilingual education, and health care passed. But why? Because they're controversial! Hispanic politicians, be they in Texas, California, Florida, or New York, have to think in terms of their total constituency—that means *gringos*, African-Americans, and everyone else. Every time they take a stand on a worthwhile project that benefits Hispanics, they're afraid they'll lose support from other groups in their district, right?"

"Yeah..." I said tentatively, nodding for him to go on.

"So what do they do?" he continued. "They avoid pushing for programs that would help us. But now you take a pyramid...Who's going to complain about that? Who would it hurt? It was such a "safe" Hispanic project that everyone jumped on the band wagon—even politicians who weren't Hispanic wanted in! These politicians argued to their more redneck supporters that the pyramid would displace Puerto Ricans and Mexicans from the big cities to the desert. That alone got us a lot of backing."

We walked back to the Bronco and Solomón started it up again. We rode in silence for a while as I thought about it all.

As we passed workers, I began to notice that there was quite a spread of people on the pyramid project. Though many were obviously Chicano, I could also see *gringos*, African Americans, Asians, you name it. It looked like a microcosm of the United Nations. I asked Zapata about this.

"Well, we had to have our token *gringos*, didn't we?" he said, smiling. "At least that's how it started. Later, when word got out that Aztecs had returned to their ancestral home, Aztlán, and were building a *pirámide*, we began to get deluged by people from all over, all wanting to be a part of it.

"They started showing up in campers, trailers and by the busloads: Hari Krishnas, gurus, pot smokers, pyramid-power believers, artists, revolutionaries, newagers, and just plain middle-class all-American folks looking for a dream to believe in."

"And?" I prodded.

"We gave it to them. Many of them are still here. The serious ones we incorporated into the work force—most of them live down at the Aztlán trailer court until the condo section of the pyramid is completed. Then they'll move in."

Condos, of course, I thought.

"Right," Zapata continued, as if reading my mind. "After the second year, we realized that even with foreign investors, we weren't going to be able to complete the pyramid at the scale we wanted."

"So our development office came up with a way to merge pyramid ownership with worker benefits without compromising our investor projects, like the hotel or the fast-food franchises. We can pay our workers less, because they own part of the *pirámide* and live on the premises."

Throughout the morning of sight-seeing, I had begun to take a real liking to Zapata. My initial surprise at finding an articulate and commanding figure in charge of what I had thought was a hoax soon turned to outright respect and admiration. Here was a man with a dream, and by damn if he wasn't making it come true.

Later, Zapata and Solomón led me through a tour of the maze-like pyramid interior. As we walked through the crowded and bustling corridors, workers and clerical staff alike called out to Zapata. Our tour was constantly interrupted as Zapata joked with the workers—he knew each one by his first name! Time and again I heard the same phrase tossed from Zapata to the workers, from the workers to Zapata, "For our children in 2025!"

2025. The completion date of the pyramid.

Throughout the afternoon of that first day, Zapata, with Solomón jovially smiling alongside, took me successively through the computer rooms and the administration offices. He showed me the now-completed daycare center for the working parents on the project. Then we took a walk through a partially completed condo section, and finally to what he was most proud of: the nearly finished kindergarten section of what was to eventually be a complete school system—from K through high school. It was there that he conferred with an engineer who pulled out blue prints for the proposed hospital, shopping center, and, of course, the radio and television studios.

"Damn," I said. "What you're building here is a virtual city!"

By now it was midafternoon, and we were sipping beers at the pyramid bar, which was located on the ground floor. They had named it "Tláloc" after the Aztec god of water. Since it was before quitting time, we were relatively alone in the cool room done up in Aztec motifs. Solomón was quick to respond to my observation.

"Of course, it is," he said. "That's what it's supposed to be: a city of our own. Don't you see that this is the only alternative we have?"

Was he getting cosmic or something? I could sense a sermon coming.

"For years we've been at the bottom of the totem pole," he continued. "We have poor education, lousy housing, no jobs. Our kids grow up in *barrios* riddled with disease, drugs and gangs. When we protest, when we ask our government to spend dollars on education, health care, programs for our youth, *¿Qué pasa?* They ignore us! As if we didn't have the rights of U.S. citizens. *¿Que no?*"

I couldn't argue much with him on that.

"So here," he went on, "we finally have a chance to do something our way. Of course, most people think it's a big joke. Building a pyramid in the middle of the desert." I sipped on my beer but said nothing. It was his rap, let him get it out.

"Damn it, Frank," he said, ignoring his beer and staring intently at me. "This pyramid is ours! We thought it up, we got the funding, we maneuvered through the ifs, buts and wherefores of this society to make it happen. Maybe it sounds like a pipe dream, but look at the alternatives open to us. The American Dream? Oh, sure, maybe a few of us—like you or me—will make it in this society. But the vast majority of our people will remain destitute. History has shown that! Our people as a whole will never have the American Dream. For them this society has become a nightmare!"

Despite his hyperbole, I could see what Solomón was getting at.

"But surely we can't drop out of society, " I ventured. "We can't ignore the country we live in."

"No," he replied, "I'm not saying we drop out. I'm saying we start with our own first; we start with something that is ours."

Zapata, who had been listening to our debate, now spoke.

"Frank, let me ask you something," he said. "Do you think that what we're doing here in the desert is different from any other human enterprise? Is it any different from landing a man on the moon, running for Congress, or writing stories for a newspaper? Are these activities any more or less real to our people than the building of this *pirámide*?"

I thought about it and nodded agreement. I saw what he meant. If anything, building the pyramid was more relevant to Chicanos than most of the things he had mentioned.

"What this pyramid is about," he continued, "is trying to make the best of our opportunities, building our own institutions, helping one another with dignity and *carnalismo*. And if we pull it off, then the world is open to us."

By his tone of voice I could tell that the sermon was over, at least for awhile. Just then, Bobby Hernández joined us and brought the Rodríguez twins and Jeannie de la Cruz with him. Boy, did she look great! Besides looking like a beauty queen, she had gotten a degree in engineering and was in charge of building the new school addition to the pyramid. Later, Rudy Vargas showed up and introduced me to his gorgeous wife María.

We ordered another round of beers and reminisced about the good old times with the Arroyo Grande Slug-

gers. The big topic of conversation, of course, was Julia
Miranda and her success in Hollywood. The big parade
honoring her down Main Street in Arroyo Grande, with
all the attendant national media coverage, had put Arroyo
Grande on the map!

Well, to make a long story short, we talked into the
night. I got drunk. The next day I was sober, if somewhat
crudo, and we talked some more. I stayed on for several
days to interview others working on the *pirámide*—now *I*
was pronouncing it in Spanish.

After a week of interviews, a lot of soul-searching,
and some lengthy long distance calls to Gloria, I agreed
to take up Zapata's offer to head the *pirámide's* promo-
tion and outreach department. Samuel Samuels at the
Times was dumbfounded.

"You're going to do *what?*" He sputtered on the telephone when I told him.

"You're crazy. You're worse than crazy. You're...Mexi-
can!"

Samuels was convinced I had been brainwashed. He
even sent me telegrams promising that he would never
again assign me to do another Hispanic story if I just
reconsidered and returned to Los Angeles.

I stayed. I got a side gig working for the local Tucson
paper until we started putting out our own *Daily Apex*.
I'm editor-and-chief now. Got quite an assistant, too,
someone from the old *barrio*. Yep, I recruited Choo Choo
Torres!

I knew that kid had talent. I was able to convince
him to join up with the *pirámide* and help out on the
paper. I expect he'll take over when I'm done, or more
likely, when I'm promoted to head up another of Zapata's expansion schemes. And yes, I still use that same
pen I fished out of Mrs. Romero's sinkhole—several cartridge replacements later.

It's been eight years since I first met Zapata, and I
suppose I'm as surprised as anybody on the success

we've been having with the *pirámide*. This year we'll have an operating budget of over $100 million.

It hasn't always been easy. We even had to stop construction a couple of times. That was, of course, before the Arabs came in with oil money. You see, some of the design spin-offs engineered by our environmentalists proved to be quite transferable to other arid regions.

Our School of Environmental Design was accredited two years ago, and it's funnier than hell to see Arabs, Africans, and Chinese taking classes taught by Chicano environmentalists.

Yes, the *pirámide* is growing. Everyone is rooting for the year 2025. What'll we do when it's finished? I don't know. Zapata has been doing a lot of research and reading into the design of space vehicles. It scares me.

One thing for sure, the *pirámide* has created quite a worldwide stir that has helped us domestically as well. Before the *pirámide,* no one knew who or what Chicanos were. Now, we have twenty reps in Congress and a half-dozen senators. This year, all the newspapers are saying that the Carillo/Kennedy ticket can't lose. Although I don't expect the descendant of a U.S. president much likes the prospect of being vice president to a Chicano...

Are we assimilating into the system, despite the Chicano nationalism that inspired the *pirámide*? Perhaps. It may be we never really had much of a choice. But at least the *pirámide* has shown what we can do with our own institutions. It's allowed us to get someplace we hadn't been before. In any case, as Solomón says, "It's a start, *ése.*"

At night, after work, I pass by the now spotlit sign that still greets you as you enter the *pirámide* grounds. I think about that quote Zapata thought to put up there so long ago: *lo que el viento se llevó, el viento devolvió.*

A *pirámide* in the desert? Who would have thought?